A WILD WILD
SPACE ADVENTURE

THE MARSHAL OF
SAMURAI MOON

By: RICHARD GRIFFITH

For Kelly, Kara, and Matt

TJ, Joey, Melinda

Chris, RJ, Ashley, and Eric

"Dreams are worth attempting"

Self-Published

COVER ILLUSTRATION BY: ME!

THE MARSHAL OF SAMURAI MOON

CHAPTER 1

The bar fell silent as the swinging doors opened and revealed the newest patron as he entered. He then stood there, letting his eyes adjust to the dim lighting, his weathered and unshaven face, was scarred but ruggedly handsome. His neo-silk shirt hung loose over his muscular frame, with the tan, custom made vest, buttoned all the way up, a silver star hung on the left breast. The cargo pants he wore, were patched, but clean, and hung over his drago-skinned boots. But what really drew everyone's eye were the blaster worn low on his right hip and his vibro-bowie blade on his left. He was the kind of a man that only fools trifled with, and fools didn't live long in this region of space.

The bar itself looked like any one of a thousand other stereotypical watering holes on this Godforsaken rock. Neo wood floors, tables, and chairs. The bar itself was a molded, poured in place, quick-crete. Sturdy, cheap, and most importantly, bullet and blaster proof. Bottles of the bar's wares were displayed along the shelves behind the bar, and tap handles boasted the local brews on tap. Brass accents were everywhere, and an old wagon wheel chandelier dared to give the place a dash of ancient legitimacy.

Somewhere stairs led to a second floor, that was supposed to be where there were rooms to rent, and instead there was company that could be purchased. In short, it was one of a dozen or so bar/brothels in town.

The stranger took it all in, every detail, as he strolled over to the bar and set his foot up on the brass rail. By the time he reached the bar, he had judged every threat, calculate where every gun was located and took in every spot where someone could remain concealed. Within seconds of setting his foot on the rail, the overly efficient bartender appeared and was dutifully taking the man's order.

"Whiskey, Talarian whiskey." The stranger ordered.

Within seconds the bartender filled a glass and set it on the bar.

"Would you like ice?" He asked as he stepped back a foot.

"No need." The stranger answered, as he downed the fiery beverage in one gulp. The burning liquid mixing pleasure with pain as it clawed its way down his throat. The man then turned his attention from his drink back to the bartender. "I'm looking for someone."

"We're not that kind of establishment." The bartender huffed stiffly in reply. "Try Miss Marzola's house down the street if you want that kind of...." The man was cut off in his tirade by the stranger grabbing him by the collar. Not only was his protest a lie, and everyone knew it, but that was not the kind of someone the man was looking for. At least not yet.

"First of all, don't insult me by telling me that it's not that kind of place." He nearly spat in the bartender's face. "Second, I'm looking for a Tishora Zakicowi." The stranger finished with a bit of a growl.

A look of indecision briefly appeared on the bartender's face, but quickly disappeared as he reached the conclusion that he would live longer if he shared any information he had, if only by a few minutes. But when one treasures every breath, minutes have a lot of value. In reply the bartender simply pointed toward a table that was half concealed in shadow.

"Who asks?" Came a demanding voice from the darkened corner of the bar. A large alien, whose true species was named the Samriza, but whose white, exaggerated featured face, traditional wearing of red, scaled armor, large bowl-shaped helmets, and tendency to carry family swords, had earned them the nickname, the Samurai. A nickname the aliens themselves fostered and revered. They had studied Earth history and knew all about the ancient warrior and their Bushido code. The aliens believed it to be an honorable comparison, so they welcomed the nickname despite its slight inaccuracies.

"You, I assume, are Zakicowi?" The stranger asked, knowing full well the answer.

"Zakicowi (Zay-Key-Cow-eye)" The alien answered with the preferred pronunciation.

"My name is Bounty-Marshal, Wyatt Toranado, and You stand charged with robbing the Wells Argo shuttle and stage." The man announced, in a loud clear voice, ignoring the correction in the pronunciation. He was so loud, in fact, that he was obviously intending the rest of the bar to bear witness to the exchange. "I'm charged with bringing you in. How that happens is up to you. Alive or dead I still get paid."

Everyone in the bar had sucked in a breath at the term Bounty-Marshal. They were a peculiar breed of occupation. Part lawman, part bounty hunter, they were usually enlisted or contracted to bring in a certain individual and then sworn in as a duly appointed law representative until such time as they were relieved or that the bounty was brought in. Wyatt was not unique in the fact that he had been given a long charter to enforce what laws he needed too in the pursuit of his duties, but it was not the norm. Still, calling Wyatt a lawman was neither technically correct nor incorrect, neither was calling him a bounty hunter.

Instead of denying the charge or blustery threats, Zakicowi launched himself in a leap at the stranger charged with his arrest. His sword was already swinging over his head in an arc that would come down square on the Bounty-Marshall's head.

Tritanium metal, was rare, expensive, and light as a feather despite the fact that a two-millimeter-thick sheet could deflect a blaster bolt or bullet and Wyatt's Neo-Neo-Stetson hat was made of it. That was not to say that the sword coming down on his head was without severe discomfort. His head rung like a bell, his eyes watered, and he could feel the start of a migraine. But he was alive and far from out of the fight.

The same could not be said of Zakicowi. His blade stopped suddenly, like it had hit a steel wall, but his body was carried by its momentum and brought to within inches of Wyatt. Close enough for Wyatt's red hot, vibro Bowie-blade to cut through the famous red scaled armor, like a laser through paper.

Wyatt was well versed in the alien anatomy of the Samurai, and knew exactly where to strike. The blade penetrated the alien's chest, but missed both sides of

Zakicowi's heart, instead it severed the conveying arteries running between the two halves. That in itself would not kill the alien immediately, but the blade didn't stop there. Instead, it plowed through the esophageal tube and into the main nerve cluster running along his spine. This caused Zakicowi to crumple to the floor, no longer able to control his body.

As the body lay on the floor, pumping out the alien's brick red life blood, Wyatt kneeled down to whisper to him.

"There is no honor in this death." He whispered to the proud alien. "Tell me where you hid the prize taken and I'll end you with honor."

"Search all of creation if you like." Came the heavily accented reply. "I'll tell you nothing."

Wyatt didn't waste his time repeating himself, instead he stood up and returned to the bar for another glass of whiskey as Zakicowi wheezed out his last few breaths on the floor.

It was all too common a story now days. A bounty hunter charged with bringing in a criminal, here on the almost lawless frontier. Blasters hung in low holsters like the six guns of old, knives settled arguments, and robbery was an everyday occurrence. Space had become the new wild west, and it was up to men like Wyatt Toranado to tame it.

Places like the saloon he had stumbled into grabbed onto the traditions of the old west with both hands. Swinging doors, wagon wheel chandeliers and cabaret stage shows were the norm around here. Even if the Shows were holographic, the lights self-contained glow cubes, and the bar and swinging doors bullet proof.

It wasn't all bad either, the return to the western philosophies. Justice was swift, but hard. People were more polite and civil to their neighbor, and the kindness in the acts of helping out a friend were outstanding. Oh there were more civilized and fancied up places, back in the core worlds, but the frontier was where people like Wyatt thrived. People even came to calling the Core, 'back east' while the frontier was often heralded as the frontier or more simply as 'the west'.

"You all saw what happened." Wyatt called out to the bar as he took a long pull from the glass in his hand. "He drew his weapon first. He attacked me from several feet away. I could have gunned him down first, but I gave him every chance to come in peacefully."

There were murmurs from around the bar, but no one directly objected to or disputed his interpretation of events.

"No one will argue that what you did was honorable." Came a new voice from across the room.

Wyatt turned and squinted into the low light in the corner, and cursed himself for missing the man/alien earlier. This could have been very ugly for him if the man in the corner had been a threat, but fortunately he was not.

"Master Kenjay." Wyatt bowed slightly to the Samurai who approached. "I did not notice you there. Greetings and salutations." Wyatt gave the traditional greeting to the alien, but what he really wanted to know was what he was doing there. The bar they were in, the *Plush Horse*, was a dive. A place for low life scum. Not a place for respectable gentleman, especially when there was a high-class entertainment house or two, not more than a kilometer or two away.

Kenjay did not wear the red scaled armor most of his fellow species preferred. He was a member of the ruling class, not one of the ruffian fighters and tradesmen that had spread across the galaxy. Instead he wore some of the finest, red, neo-silk robes, woven Ebony Root sandals, and gold trimmed robe ties. He also carried a gold handled sword, hand forged in the finest traditional house and constructed from only the best and most secret materials. It was not just decorative, that sword. If Kenjay carried one from that legendary house, he was a master with it.

"You gave him every chance." Kenjay observed. "He chose his fate."

"I am sorry to burden your eyes with the death of a kinsman." Wyatt consoled in the tradition manner when on had to kill one of Kenjay's species.

"I appreciate the gesture." Kenjay replied, honestly. "But no tears will be shed at this pirate's passing. The Wells Argo stage he robbed affected me and my business as well. I only wish you would have succeeded in gaining the location from him before he expired."

"My apologies, but the situation was not conducive to a long interrogation." Wyatt informed him. "Now if you'll excuse me, I have to arrange to deliver the shell of Zakicowi." It would be an insult to call it a body. The Samurai did not believe that a body was anything of value after death, especially when one died in defiance of the law. Only the shell remained as the spirit had departed.

Kenjay bowed indicating that he was no longer concerned or interested in continuing the conversation. Not that his displeasure at being dismissed would matter that much to Wyatt. Still, Kenjay could make his life difficult if he wished, so it was better to not upset the man.

Kenjay then walked up to the bar and pressed several credits into the proprietor's hand. He didn't say another word, but his implication was clear. He was paying for the rest of Wyatt's drinks and entertainment for the night. The implication that Wyatt was under Kenjay's protection was not lost on the patrons.

Wyatt wasn't sure why Kenjay was taking such a keen interest, but he was certain he wasn't going to like the answers when they revealed themselves. Still, a free night out was a free night. Whiskey always tended to taste better when someone else was picking up the tab.

It took only a few minutes for the official local law enforcement to take possession of the samurai's shell and for the bio bots to clean up the floor. After that a few statements were taken and payment doled out for the bounty on Zakicowi. It was an all too common exchange in this near lawless frontier. But so many, humans and alien alike, wouldn't have it any other way.

CHAPTER 2

Wyatt awoke to a pounding door and an aching head. Maybe it was the other way around. He also had some company in bed with him, that he would have to shoo away quickly, lest she get the wrong idea about his intentions. That little scenario seemed unlikely as the women who tended to end up with someone like him were either professionals or were used to the one night stand, kind of guy.

There was the not so minor detail, of just who's room he was in. He calculated that he was upstairs in the very bar he had dispatched one criminal Samurai in, the previous night. But he was not absolutely certain of that. Evidently the combination of Kenjay's hospitality and having just gotten a big bounty had combined in a celebration replete with whiskey and poor decisions. Not that, looking at the uncovered female in the bed with him, she was a bad decision, he just wished he could remember the good time he must have had.

The pounding on the door resumed anew, albeit a little bit louder this time. So Wyatt, convinced he couldn't ignore it, got up, grabbed his blaster from his holster, and opened up the door.

"Mister Toranado." The beautiful, tall, redhaired woman began, pushing him out of the way and entering his room without an invitation, began. "I shall be needing a minute of your time. My name is Sonnet Melville and you're…oh my god…you're naked."

She had stormed in so quickly that she hadn't taken stock of the fact that he was not in condition, or attire, in which to entertain guests.

Wyatt fought back a smile at her reaction, it wouldn't do to put a crack in his tough guy persona and let her know that she had amused him in some way. Better to play it as the irritated hard ass.

Miss Melville turned a look away as quickly as she could. Even so, she would have admitted, if forced, that his physical prowess was worthy of a second, or even third, glance. He was typical tough guy handsome, with a strong chin, chiseled face, rough looking short brown hair and enough scars to accent, but not detract. He was also fairly tall, and stocky, for a society that had become very automated, and had thus shrunk in size.

"You can turn around Miss Melville." Wyatt yawned. "I haven't got anything you haven't seen before, and probably in less than spectacular proportions. Besides, your eyes haven't left the mirror you are looking into since you turned to face away from me."

She blushed noticeably as she sheepishly turned around. Yes, he had nothing new to look at, but she would argue that there was nothing wrong with his 'proportions', as he put it.

"Mister Toranado," She began with a bit of a sputter as she turned to face him. "Perhaps it would be better if we put off our conversation until another time." It was then that she noticed the naked female still in the bed. "Perhaps when you are alone."

"You've already ruined my plans to sleep in and start my day by accomplishing a whole lot of nothing." He grumped as he placed his blaster back in its holster. He then walked over to the basin and swallowed a combination of pain pills and hangover killers. The second item being the ones he felt were the pinnacle of human medical technology. It was all downhill from there, if you asked him. "So state your piece or leave me the hell alone. I already got it figured that you want me for work, which is my least favorite thing to do."

She straightened herself and cleared her throat. She was determined and was not going to be intimidated by his stance, reputation, or bluster.

"Very well." She began, pacing in the small space she was allotted. "My name, as I said before, is Sonnet Melville. My father is Copernicus Melville."

"Copernicus Melville." Wyatt repeated as he slid on his pants. "The guy that discovered the location of the lost *Princess of Mars* space-liner all those years ago? The ship that went missing with a small fortune of blue gold on board?"

"That would be correct." She confirmed for him. "He used his share of the salvage to provide rather well for us over the years." She added, with a touch of sadness.

Wyatt looked her over again. Her long red hair was bright and healthy, she was lovely to look at with a symmetrical face and well-toned body. But she wasn't dressed like someone with a lot of money. Her clothes were off the rack, her fingers showed signs of working, and her nails were done, but were probably done by her. She did, however, have a pair of custom made, draco-skinned boots, like his, that bulged slightly. Which usually indicated that she had a weapon concealed in them.

She noticed him sizing her up and quickly continued.

"We lived well, Mister Toranado, not extravagantly." She seemed to hold her hands away from her sides to give him a better look at what she wore. "My father used the money, not only to support a family, but also to continue to search for other lost treasures. He was obsessed with it, but not very successful. He had finally reached the point where he only had enough left for one more expedition."

"Which was?" Wyatt, felt he already knew the answer to his question, but wanted her to confirm it. He wasn't a man who lived on assumptions.

"The Wells Argo stage." She revealed, confirming his suspicions.

He nodded, as he came to terms with the fact that this would indeed mean more work, and not the kind that he was necessarily used to.

"That ship was hijacked by Tishora Zakicowi over a s-year ago, and nobody heard anything about it." He sighed wearily. "Now I meet three people with a connection to it in less than sixteen hours. What gives? Why now?"

"First tell me what you know about the stage?" She challenged. Crossing her arms and tapping her foot slightly. Just like an old schoolmarm listening to a student recite a lesson.

He just sighed and shrugged. It was obvious he wasn't going to be getting back into bed so he might as well play along.

"Wells Argo, and company, decide to shift a good portion of their financial operations to be closer to the mining and excavations in the Echo quadrant. Specifically, to be closer to the mines on Ark 3." He began his exposition as he knew it. "Tishora Zakicowi, sees it as an opportunity for some ill-gotten gains and organizes a little pirate party to meet them while they are on route, somewhere near the Tristar system. A place where sensors are notoriously unreliable.

"He's in for a bit of a surprise when he finds out that Well Argo has tripled the amount of sting-ships in escort. What was supposed to be a simple operation becomes a fiasco, leading to the destruction of almost every pirate within five quadrants. Making the galaxy safer, but costing Wells a ship and all the credits and credit servers on board. Zakicowi, gets away with the stage and the loot. Most, if not all, of his comrades wind up dead. Notable exceptions being Curzo, Zakicowi, and their crews, and I end up taking down Zakicowi."

"And due to your overzealous actions, the whereabouts of the stage may never be known." She sighed and tapped her foot slightly.

"Bringing in Zakicowi was my job." Wyatt protested. "Not finding a lost ship."

"Something I would like to change." She finally admitted.

CHAPTER 3

"Excuse me?" Wyatt wasn't sure he had heard her correctly, but had a sinking feeling that he had. The grimace on his face betrayed his poker player persona.

"I would like you to assist me in finding the Wells Argo stage." She confirmed. "More specifically the *Western Rose*, as the stage was officially named.

"You are correct, in *most* everything you said. Zakicowi did unite the pirates for a bold strike. They arrived and found triple the security sting ships that they thought they should have. But not just because they were moving financial headquarters. No, Wells Argo tripled their security because the ship was carrying a large amount of a rare element. One that could revolutionize space travel, communication and even weaponry, that element being Baryonic Dark Matter."

"Come again?" Wyatt raised an eyebrow and searched his chemistry knowledge to see if he could make sense of what she was talking about.

"Baryonic dark matter has been around for centuries, but never in large quantities." She explained. "Even now it is exceedingly rare. Recently, scientists have discovered that it contains vast amounts of power if tapped into correctly. For instance, a power rod the size of your pinky, could power your ship for a hundred years or more."

"So the amount the *Rose* is carrying could be worth?" Wyatt asked, an eyebrow betraying a bit of interest.

"I am unsure of the amounts, as Wells Argo has been very tight lipped about it." She revealed. "But if the amounts rumored to be onboard are anywhere close to accurate, we could be looking at the annual wealth of an entire system. And not a small system."

Wyatt's eyes didn't betray him, but his brain was spinning with possibilities. Even a small percentage of that amount would be more than he had ever made in his life. More than he could really conceive of. Certainly more than he could ever use. That was an idea that appealed to him a great deal. He just hoped that his poker face held out this time.

"Just what makes you think that I can help you in this treasure hunt?" Wyatt asked, only to be interrupted by another knock at the door.

Both he and Sonnet looked at each other, and she shrugged to indicate that she didn't know who it was, or what was going on either. Wyatt then walked over to the door, blaster back in his hand, and opened it.

"Master Kenjay." Wyatt greeted as he took in the sight of the alien aristocrat before him. "Why am I not surprised to see you?"

"Because you are a perceptive man." Kenjay answered. "A naked one to be sure, but still perceptive." Kenjay was able to stifle a chuckle at taking in the unclothed ruffian, but still managed a wry smile across his alien face.

Wyatt looked down and finally grabbed his pants off the bed. The woman laying there stirred, but did not rouse.

"What can I do for you Master Kenjay?" Wyatt asked politely as he slipped his legs into his trousers.

"As you are busy, entertaining multiple females." Kenjay began, looking at the two women. "Perhaps I should return at a more opportune time."

"Don't bother." Sonnet snapped at the alien. "Mister Toranado is otherwise engaged, by me. Employment wise, that is."

"Is this statement accurate? Mister Toranado?" Kenjay gave Wyatt the eye, which was odd with his black on black iris and pupil.

"As of yet," Wyatt began slowly. "I have not agreed to anything. Miss Melville here, has just been giving me some background."

"On the *Western Rose*, I assume?" Kenjay surmised correctly. "The missing Wells Argo stage."

"With all due respect, Master Kenjay." Wyatt began as he finished buckling on his gun and knife belt. All he needed now was his shirt, if he could find it. "I can no more discuss the lady's business with you, than I could discuss yours with her. Discretion is a bit of a must in my racket."

Kenjay nodded and bowed slightly in understanding and respect.

"I am willing to openly discuss my offer with you and the lady, if she is willing to do the same." Kenjay then looked down at the still sleeping woman on the bed. "But the female in the bed, must depart."

It took a few minutes to get the woman woken up enough to get her things and get out, but Wyatt was firm with her and gave her a good tip as incentive to hasten her departure.

"Now that we are all alone, at least all the interested parties are here and isolated," Kenjay mused, as he paced around the small room. "We may begin in earnest.

"I understand that Miss Melville has made you an offer, but I doubt that she has explained to you why you are so important."

Melville opened her mouth to protest, but Wyatt held up his hand to silence her.

"To be honest, we've only gotten to a little bit of background about the job." Wyatt explained. "We haven't even gotten to a formal offer of employment as of yet. To be honest I don't even know if I'm going to take any jobs at the moment. The monies from my last bounty should keep me comfortable for a while."

"True." Kenjay replied. "But you would have to return to work eventually. The job of finding and salvaging the *Western Rose*, would provide enough for a permanent retirement, if you so wished."

"I'm not exactly a salvage expert." Wyatt protested. "That being the case, I'm not sure why you both want me."

"There are several reasons." Kenjay began, cutting off Melville as she tried to interject. "One of which is that you have a ship designed to keep a low profile. There is also the fact that you are well known for your ability to defend yourself in both space battles and on the ground. Then, there is the main reason that requires you alone."

Wyatt couldn't dispute what Kenjay was saying, but gave him the eye just the same. He was well known for his ability as a fighter, both in the cockpit and on the ground. That came courtesy of the military training he had as a member of the Special Insertion and Tactical Extraction Unit (SITE-U). He had seen action many times, but had also learned the hard way that bad intelligence could get men killed. Resentment toward senior officers that had issued orders based on bad intel was the reason he had walked away from, what was left of, his team and gone into business for himself.

"What, exactly, requires me alone?" Wyatt finally asked.

"We believe that Tishora Zakicowi, was in possession of coordinates that could lead us to the *Western Rose*." Melville revealed. Jumping in ahead of Kenjay. "Perhaps not the actual location itself, but clues that could help us find it."

"And as part of my people's traditions, you are the only one that can claim Zakicowi's personal effects." Kenjay finished, pretending not to notice the interruption. "You ended his life and brought him to justice. All that he possessed on him at that moment, now belong to you. Technically you now own all of his property in our home system, but my people would never let an outsider lay claim to our home soil, regardless of tradition. What he had on his person, however, is a different matter. Even his ship, is now legally your property."

"What about challenges from kin?" Wyatt inquired, not wanting to get into the middle of a feud.

"They may protest to the taking of his ship." Kenjay admitted. "But not to anything he had on him. Our people will never go that far into breaking with tradition. Even staking a claim on his ship would take time and be frowned upon. It is also doubtful that they would want to get involved, given the nature of his profession and how that tarnished his family's reputation, they probably will not challenge your possession of his vessel. They will, instead, prefer to act as if it and he, never existed. Less shame on the family name that way."

"What about his crew?" Wyatt was doubtful that pirates would care very much about tradition and honor.

"They will probably strip what they want from his ship, if given the opportunity, and leave a barely operable hulk. They are an uncouth mix of human and samurai alike, and not very concerned with the honor of their houses." Kenjay made a disgusted noise at that. Clearly the thought of those of his race being so unconcerned with the honor of their clans upset him. "Even they, however, would not break tradition where the body is concerned. There is also the fact that most of the crew were disposed of after the Rose was hidden or killed in taking it as a prize. I do not believe that the few that remain, are yet aware of Tishora Zakicowi's demise."

"So you have them under surveillance." Wyatt deduced correctly, which was confirmed by a nod from Kenjay.

"I am operating under the assumption, and I'm sure Master Kenjay is as well, That Zakicowi was so concerned about the location of the *Rose* that he kept the coordinates to it on him at all times." Melville stated firmly. She doubted that he would have left something that important on his ship, but one never knew for certain.

"Miss Melville is correct." Kenjay confirmed. "But to be safe, I have placed his ship under guard. I am, the expression is, I believe, covering all the bases."

A thought then occurred to Wyatt. One that he wasn't sure how Kenjay was going to react to, but he was going to put it out there anyway.

"So that is why you were in the bar last night." Wyatt finally had his lightbulb moment. "You were there to try and convince Zakicowi to give you the location to the Rose, and failing that you were going to challenge him."

Kenjay did not answer, but simply nodded and bowed deeply to indicate that he was indeed, guilty as charged. Not that such a thing would have been frowned upon in either human or samurai society. Kenjay had already stated that the taking of the Rose had affected him professionally. That would be an honor bound reason to challenge Zakicowi and take his revenge. Such things were uncommon, but happened often enough to be general knowledge.

"So are you here to challenge me to take possession of Zakicowi's effects yourself?" Wyatt twitched a little toward his blaster, but didn't make an outright play for it.

"I considered such a thing." Kenjay admitted. "But the same rules of possession do not translate into your culture. I might not be able to take charge of Zakicowi's possessions like you could. Also, having a person that is good in a fight on my side, might be a good thing. There is also the fact that my race, is not always the most welcome everywhere in the galaxy, so having a human I could trust along might be beneficial."

"How do you know you can trust me?" Wyatt inquired, with genuine curiosity.

"There is, to date, no record of you ever crossing anyone once you have a contract." Kenjay returned easily, indicating that he had done his homework on Wyatt. "There have been a few occasions where you have failed to fulfil your contract, but none where you intentionally betrayed anyone for money. For a human, you have an incredible sense of honor."

It was true. Wyatt had never crossed anyone when it came to his work. He had the occasional bounty slip through his fingers and beat him to a non-extradition sector, but he had never actually taken a dime he didn't earn. Well, there was the time he let Wilber McGintry go free, but his daughter and Wyatt had had a thing going, and he couldn't bear to see her lose him. Of course, no one knew about that either.

"So both of you, tell me exactly what you want of me." Wyatt finally found his shirt and finished getting dressed.

CHAPTER 4

Kenjay, Melville and Wyatt had moved the location of their meeting to a place that was considered more secure and less likely to have any prying ears around. Instead, they gathered in one of Kenjay's working offices. Not one of the lavish ones he used for dealing with the VIPs he often hobnobbed with, but still one that was comfortable and functional.

It had originally been Wyatt's suggestion that they move the negotiations and meet up after he had a chance to shower and freshen up. He had at least one experience before where a hotel room had turned out to be bugged and his quarry was warned off. Still, even though he agreed to wait and trusted Wyatt, Kenjay had not moved farther away from him than right outside the bathroom door. Melville seemed to be less possessive, but he was certain that she had kept Kenjay in sight at all times as well.

"So what exactly, is the deal you two are offering me?" Wyatt began as he plopped down into one of the overly comfortable chairs.

"The two of us?" Melville repeated, shooting a nervous glance over at Kenjay.

"It is obvious that the two of you are after the same thing." Wyatt started laying out. "I'm willing to bet that each of you have information on the ship that would be beneficial to its recovery. So let's put our cards on the table. For instance, what did your father know before he disappeared?"

A slight look of shock came over Melville's face as she fumbled a bit.

"I never said my father was missing." She stammered.

"You said that he had the resources for one last expedition." Wyatt started to lay out. "He went on that expedition, I remember reading about it. So if you are here looking for the ship, and he isn't, that means he's missing. You're hoping to find, not only the ship, but also your father."

She sat back into her chair, but said nothing for a long time. She was obviously arguing with herself as to what she needed to tell him.

"My father disappeared six months ago." She finally answered softly. "He made me copies of all of his research and charts before he left, and confided in me the most logical location of the stage. After that it was 'bye bye pumpkin' and he was off. Another wild goose chase."

Wyatt nodded, but pretended to not be too interested in her missing father. Why let her know she was pulling at his heartstrings?

"Master Kenjay, you said you had business reasons for finding the stage." Wyatt referred to their conversation at the bar. "Or to be more precise, you said that it affected your business."

"I am, was, heavily invested in the cargo of the stage." Kenjay revealed. "It was to go to one of my research stations. One that was close to the element mines.

The combination of the two elements was necessary so one of them had to be moved. I was under the impression that Wells Argo could be trusted to deliver my cargo intact. It cost me millions, but would have been worth it, had the research panned out."

"So to put this a bluntly as possible. You both want to hire me, you both have information that would make this easier to accomplish, and you're both broke." Wyatt was making a calculated guess on that last part.

Both Kenjay and Melville tried to look affronted at that last part. Kenjay had a reputation as a highly successful business man to protect and project. As for Melville, well, she just didn't like being pegged like he had done.

"Miss Melville there, said that her father only had the funds for one more expedition." Wyatt reasoned. "As for you, Master Kenjay, you wouldn't have been willing to face down a ruffian in public had you had another choice. It is beneath your station, as it were. You both need this and it looks like you both need me. I'm willing to bet that the both of you together couldn't charter a ship without putting it on credit."

"You are essentially correct." Kenjay admitted, even though it grated on him to do so. "I also calculated that you would also want to use your own ship, the *Stallion*, or Zakicowi's ship and would therefore be cheaper to hire if you were part of the salvage company. You have the advantage of being an independent pilot with access to your own vessels. Most pilots work for companies that own their freighters. They have a corporation to answer to, you just have yourself."

Even Sonnet Melville, nodded slowly after a moment.

"Well this is a position I rarely find myself in." Wyatt chuckled. "I have all the resources and you have the information to make this little expedition worth it. Usually it's a matter of my having the expertise and my client having the funds. The question now is, since I don't really need the work at the moment, what is my motivation here?"

"The monies we are talking about here, is…." Kenjay began.

"Is more than I could ever spend." Wyatt finished for him. "So what, exactly, do I need you two for?"

"I am willing to wager," Kenjay began. "That both Miss Melville and myself are in possession of certain details and clues to the whereabouts of the *Western Rose*. I was guessing, before her revelation, that she is in possession of much of her father's research on the subject. I, on the other hand, have the cultural knowledge to interpret what we learn from Zakicowi's possessions. I am also, not without certain contacts when it comes to disposal of the cargo."

"So she has the information to make finding the ship probable, while you have the information to make finding the ship profitable." Wyatt observed.

Both of them simply nodded in reply.

Wyatt fought with his inner self. He didn't like to work, period. It then became a question of putting off something he didn't like or having the possibility of putting it off indefinitely. Lazy now or lazy later. In these cases, lazy now usually won out, but the possibility of there being a, never having to work again, in there, was very tempting.

"I cannot do anything to convince you to do anything you don't want to." Kenjay began as he started to rise. "But I can promise you this. Once word gets out, and it will, you will have a target on your back from people who will see your demise as a way to get to Zakicowi's information. If we help each other, you may be able to put those kinds of people far enough behind you to keep you safe.

"There will also be the matter, of being a partner with the house of Kenjay. Something that may open certain doors for you in the future."

"As for me." Sonnet began, as she too rose to leave. "I can offer you nothing but a partnership, a chance at riches beyond your imagination, and my gratitude. I can also offer you the possibility of providing closure for a concerned and grieving daughter."

Wyatt nodded at that and rose as well. He recognized that the meeting was over, and got the hint to get moving. He was conflicted in his thought process at the moment, and he would need some time to process the information he had just gotten, and do some research on his potential partners. Master Kenjay, even though he was an alien from a more secretive culture, was actually less of a wild card than Miss Melville. No, Wyatt needed information.

"I will consider your offer." Wyatt finally stated. "I will let you know by fifteen hundred this afternoon." He then turned slightly to address Kenjay. "As I recall, that is the earliest I could lay claim to Zakicowi's remains anyway."

"Very true." Kenjay replied. "There must be a time of stillness to allow the spirit to vacate the carcass." He still wouldn't call it a body. That would give the criminal too much respect. He would use a lot of terms for it, but not body. "One thing you should know, is that after you claim

Zakicowi's effects, you will be responsible for the disposal of his shell."

Wyatt considered this for a moment and came up with an idea on that point. It would be tradition to have the body sent back to the family, which could be very expensive, but there was also a counter tradition for one that was considered an explorer, artist, poet or some of the other professions in Samurai culture. It was the explorer occupation that Wyatt was most interested in at the moment. He just had to convince Kenjay that the title fit.

"Would it be safe to say that as an expert in hostile ship acquisitions," A nice way to say pirate. "That Zakicowi would have visited regions of space that no one had ever been to before?"

Kenjay thought for a moment, as he was blindsided by this seemingly random direction of the conversation. It would not have been a question he would have actively pondered before, but it was probably arguably true.

"I would say that it would be safe to say, that Zakicowi visited and hid in secret locations." Kenjay agreed. "Otherwise the Wells Argo stage would probably have been found already."

"Very well." Wyatt stroked his chin in thought. He really was still on the fence about the goose chase he was being lured into, but the possible rewards were very tempting indeed. "Let us adjourn for now, and meet up at the regional clerk's office at fifteen hundred. There I will officially claim the remains of Zakicowi."

Both Melville and Kenjay nodded at Wyatt, who left the office first. He didn't exactly trust the people at his back, but they had every reason to keep him alive for now. He wasn't worried about getting a knife between the shoulder blades, yet. He would, however, have to prepare himself for the eventual double cross if he did decide to throw in with these two. He would be pleasantly surprised if it didn't happen, but better, as Kenjay said, cover all the bases.

CHAPTER 5

Wyatt, who had retreated to a local cyber café to use the web, looked up from the research that he had been doing, just in time to notice that he needed to leave. He had asked everyone to meet at the Regional Clerk's office at a fifteen-hundred and he had just enough time to make it if he left now. He hated it when people were late, so he was always careful about being on time himself.

Soon they were all gathered around the office, filling out paperwork and wading through bureaucratic red tape. It would turn out that claiming the carcass was less paperwork than being a witness to it. Melville and Kenjay, as witnesses, were buried in a larger mountain of affidavits and affirmations than Wyatt was. Something that amused Wyatt to no end.

Finally, they were presented with the personal effects of the deceased. The carcass would be delivered to Zakicowi's former vessel, and now Wyatt's new ship, the next day.

"How much of this do you need?" Wyatt inquired of Master Kenjay as they looked over the items surrendered to them. "I know that the family would want his ceremonial armor back, and anything related to his house, will they require his sword as well?"

"Definitely not!" Kenjay snapped most resolutely. "Returning the sword of a defeated foe would be an insult to the surviving members of his house. His armor, however, is another matter. It represents the defense of his own, and still bears honor. Also, any banners or flags aboard his vessel should be returned. Mind you, that this is all voluntary as you have legitimate claim over everything that was his. It would simply be a nice gesture on your part, and ensure that no family members come seeking these items."

"Why is the return of the sword regarded as an insult?" Wyatt asked, genuinely confused.

"Ordinarily it would not be." Kenjay explained, more patiently now. "A soldier fallen in battle or a guardsman dying defending his charge is usually a point of honor and the sword is revered. In this case, Zakicowi was engaged in criminal designs and fell attacking a keeper of the peace. Also, he fell in battle with a human, no less. Something my species regards as somewhat of an insult. You are an inferior race, to many of my countrymen. No offense intended."

"None taken." Wyatt nodded to his alien educator. "Except the part about me being a Peace Keeper. I'm basically just a bounty hunter."

"You brought a law breaker to justice." Kenjay snickered a little. "My people will distinguish no difference between you and a lawman in this case. Despite any insult, you may feel about it."

"Less of an insult, and more of a discomfort." Wyatt explained. "People always assume that if I'm connected to law enforcement, I must be the good guy. But let me assure you, if you're looking for a hero, I ain't it."

Kenjay nodded in understanding. They all then turned their attention to the objects on the table before them.

Sonnet looked over some of the smaller items, then picked up a dark ebony root bracelet.

"This is beautiful." She gasped as she turned it over in her hand.

"Ebony root." Kenjay nodded appreciating her eye for beauty. "It is one of the most exquisite woods of my home world. It catches the light so perfectly. Almost all of my kind carry some small form of it. Usually as a necklace or bracelet."

"May I?" She asked, Wyatt, indicating that she wanted to try it on.

"Go ahead." He encouraged. "It's all got to go with us anyway. Might as well travel on your wrist."

She slipped it on and admired it for few moments. For a simple wooden ring, it reflected the light and shined beautifully. It was truly a work of master craftsmanship.

"I think we should make detailed scans of the armor, inside and out, before we send them off." Wyatt offered. "Just in case there are any clues hidden on it."

"What's this?" Sonnet held up a small tube. It contained a miniscule amount of fluid inside it, which was a silver in color.

"Looks like mercury." Wyatt observed as he squinted at the vial she held.

Kenjay too, looked it over, but shrugged as to its meaning.

There were some other objects among the effects that were possibly of interest to them. Some computer chips, which might have some information and even a rolled up smart pad, which needed to be charged before they could get any information from it.

Wyatt then wrapped things up by making arrangements for Zakicowi's armor to be scanned, and then returned to his family. All honor would be given to the presentation and everyone should be satisfied.

"So have you made a final decision?" Kenjay inquired, his clay-like face doing its best to raise an eyebrow. Even Sonnet gave him an almost pleading look.

"I have a proposal." Wyatt began. "Ten percent of the total value of the cargo, a fifty thousand flat fee that will be paid regardless of the expedition's success, that's from each of you, and I keep Zakicowi's ship."

"Ten percent seems excessive, considering the value of the cargo." Sonnet blurted out, before Kenjay could stop her.

"I have the resources, the bulk of the information, and the skills necessary to pull this thing together. In fact, I now want twenty percent." Wyatt gave her a level look that would have wilted fake flowers.

"I find twenty percent agreeable." Kenjay voiced quickly. "You are, of course, correct in your assessment of the situation. Both Miss Melville and I have pieces of the puzzle, but you have the most complete image."

Sonnet quickly nodded in concurrence this time, and made a mental note to think her objections through a little more, before she voiced them.

Wyatt then recommended that the group make their way to his new ship, calling it Zakicowi's ship would be an insult, and look it over for more clues. As such they hurried from the soon to be closing government office and out into the street. They had a little way to walk, but not enough to worry about catching a cab.

"I'll have a friend of mine meet us at the vessel." Wyatt voiced as the trio exited the building with a large box loaded on a hover pallet following them. "He's a smith and can get us access."

"Do you trust him?" Sonnet asked, giving him a worried glance.

"As much as I can trust anybody." Wyatt grinned a little. "Which in this business ain't much. But he believes that he's just there to help me with standard salvage, so it should be fine."

"Wyatt Toranado!" A voice yelled out from behind them.

The group turned to see three samurai standing in the middle of the street. People around them, recognized a challenge when they heard one, and quickly made themselves scarce.

Wyatt squinted at the armor the men were wearing. It was the same traditional red, but with black and gold accents on the arms and legs. Two of the flanking aliens held their swords high, while the center on simply rested his hand on the hilt of his, undrawn. Their clay looking faces were contorted, in what Wyatt interpreted, in a mask of rage.

"I am Senior Guardsman Torka." The center samurai roared. "And I challenge you to the right of Zakicowi's property."

In an instant, Kenjay had drawn his own sword and stood ready, while Sonnet had produced a blaster that Wyatt hadn't even been aware that she was hiding but was probably the bulge he noticed in her boot earlier.

"My choice of weapons?" Wyatt replied, sounding somewhat bored by the challenge.

A confused look crossed Torka's face. He clearly had no idea what Wyatt was referring to.

"In my culture," Wyatt explained. "The challenged man chooses the weapons of the duel."

Torka clearly did not expect this. His thoughts were that he would either be fighting, dead, or walking away with forfeited goods by now. Having a discussion was the last thing he was prepared for.

"In my culture, duels are resolved at the point of a sword." Torka grumbled. "It is the tradition of our race."

"I'm not of your race." Wyatt smiled. He then drew his blaster in a motion that was smooth and faster than a man could blink. He squeezed off three shots in a spread that was perfectly placed.

The two aliens to each side of Torka were struck square in the face. Their husks, crumpling to the ground, like puppets who had just had the strings cut. Torka was struck in the center of his chest, the blaster bolt burning through his armor and penetrating deep into his chest.

There was no movement from anyone for several seconds, as shock penetrated Wyatt's companions, and Wyatt just waited to see if anyone got back up. After it became clear that no one was, Wyatt cautiously strode over to Torka.

The alien was still alive as Wyatt stood over him, but he was fading.

"You have no honor sir." Torka mumbled to the bounty hunter.

"Never said I did." Wyatt replied, and then fired another bolt right between the dying alien's eyes.

"What have you done!" Kenjay voiced through gritted teeth. "He issued a challenge. There is no honor in killing him like you did."

"I answered his challenge." Wyatt reasoned. "I just chose the weapon I was most comfortable with. Besides, Torka here didn't take a minor detail into account."

"Which was?" Kenjay demanded.

"Computer, call up the bounty list." Wyatt spoke into his wrist computer. A small, but powerful computer that was interactive, had its own dull AI and could do almost everything from surf the interweb to auto pilot Wyatt's ship. Wyatt often referred to it as Al, but for now, calling it computer would do.

In response to Wyatt's command, a project image appeared before the group. Wyatt then scrolled through the Bounty List and pulled up the image of Torka.

"Wanted dead or alive." Wyatt pointed out, with a bit of a scowl aimed at Kenjay. "Murder, rape, piracy, and pillaging. He was one of Zakicowi's crew. His second in command if I'm right."

Kenjay's anger subsided. He still believed that an honorable challenge required an honorable response, but he could now see Wyatt's argument had validity. Had Wyatt shot the alien in the back, he still would have been justified in bringing in this criminal. It was one of those hairsplitting arguments that meant nothing here in the wild, untamed, regions of space.

"Did you not consider that he might have had information about the whereabouts of the Wells Argo stage?" Sonnet demanded as she pulled up her dress and holstered her firearm into her boot. Wyatt took a moment to not only note the location of her weapon but also to admire the shapely leg to which it was attached.

"If he had that information he would have already gone after it." Wyatt returned. "He was looking for the same clues we are. That is why he needed the possessions of Zakicowi."

Sonnet pouted for a moment as she looked for something else to be angry about. Truth of it was that she was blowing off steam from being so frightened just a moment before. It was true that her father had taught her how to handle a blaster and how to defend herself, but that was a far cry from it actually happening. A person in her position, would never experience the type of combat that Wyatt and Kenjay seemed to be so comfortable with. The truth was that it was only Wyatt who was comfortable in combat. Kenjay had trained for it, quite hard in fact, but he was relatively inexperienced in it.

Since the commotion had subsided, people were beginning to filter back out into the street. Sirens of Peacekeeper's vehicles could be heard heading their direction.

"Perhaps we should make ourselves less visible?" Kenjay offered as he indicated that they should leave.

"Nope." Wyatt replied, putting his blaster on safe and securing it in his holster. "I've been caught gunning these guys down on at least three different scanners. If I run, one, I'll never be able to claim the bounty, and two, I'll just get arrested. I've got to stay and give the Peacekeepers a report."

"Your bounty can't amount to anything compared to what the salvage of the *Western Rose* is worth." Sonnet griped.

"And nothing is worth anything, if I end up in prison for walking away from this shooting." Wyatt returned rather harshly. "So if you two want to walk away and meet me at the ship, I'm not gonna stop you. But I'm giving my statement to the local lawmen and collecting the bounty on this man, and his cohorts if they are on the list."

Kenjay sighed, but resigned himself to remaining where they were. Sonnet likewise came to the conclusion that they should do this Wyatt's way.

It didn't actually take very long for the report to be filed. Wyatt's account was backed up by what the local scanners had caught, the scanners being positioned throughout the town for this very type of thing. When Wyatt returned, if he returned, his bounty would be waiting for him and his claim to their possessions would be ready, if he wanted them.

CHAPTER 6

Wyatt had been thoughtful enough to com his friend and let him know what had happened, and that they were going to be delayed in their arrival. Still, the smith was waiting for them when they arrived.

"Hey Wyatt." Alexander Kirby called out as the bounty hunter approached.

"Kirby." Wyatt nodded as he firmly shook the man's hand. "It's good to see you."

Sonnet gave the man a suspicious look, but even she had to admit that the elderly black man standing before them had the gentlest brown eyes she had ever seen. His hair betrayed his age, as it was heavily grey and beginning to recede. In a day and age when the average lifespan was three-hundred-years, she would have to guess that this man was on the frontside of two-hundred.

"Better to see you." Kirby replied honestly. "Especially when I know you've got money to pay for my services."

Wyatt reared back in mock offence.

"When have I ever not paid?" Wyatt demanded to know.

"Oh, you've paid." Kirby admitted. "Not always on time, sometimes you have even taken years, but at least you've paid."

The two then laughed. It was true that Wyatt had not always been prompt, but he was a man who firmly believed that one paid their debts. Several times he had to make special trips to do it, or pay in ways other than standard credits, but he always squared up.

"So this the job you told me about?" Kirby stated the obvious as they stood in front of Wyatt's new ship. "She's bigger than I thought."

Wyatt too, was surprised at the sheer size of the vessel. She was a Type V Victor class Corvette. Almost eighty years old, but solid as a rock. Most of this type started out as medium range escorts and resupply ships, but when they were retired, they were stripped of their armaments and refitted as freighters. Zakicowi had obviously refitted his ship with the original weaponry and used it for piracy. It was something that Wyatt would have to address if he was going to make her legal again.

"Yeah." Wyatt breathed out impressed. "She's just on the edge of what can safely be landed dirtside. Fully loaded, I'll bet she's a bear to get into space again."

"Not a problem for most pirates." Kirby chuckled. "They only worry about landing full of stolen goods. Not taking off with them."

"What's her name?" Wyatt turned to ask Master Kenjay, as he was not that familiar with the alien's native writing.

"She is *Queen's Revenge*." He answered, running a hand across the hull in an almost loving way. "Named for our Revered Queen Torozito, no doubt. She had commissioned pirates all over the galaxy during the great rebellion."

Wyatt racked his brain for a moment, searching his memory for what he knew about the great rebellion Kenjay was referring to. Approximately five hundred s-years ago a section of the Samriza empire decided it wanted independence. At first there was a long cold war, which soon became a trade war, which eventually evolved into an actual shooting war. Millions of Kenjay's people were killed, and the empire eventually reunited. It was a dark period in the Samriza history, but no darker than a lot of periods in any culture's past.

"Good to know he recognized himself as a pirate." Wyatt mused. "By the way, Kirby, this is Master Kenjay. He's one of my business partners on this little venture."

Kirby managed a traditional bow toward the wealthy alien who returned it in kind.

"A pleasure to make your acquaintance." The mechanic greeted sincerely.

"A pleasure to make yours as well." Kenjay replied. He then looked the dark-skinned man up and down. "I have always found it interesting how you humans have evolved to look so different from one another. It is a refreshing change from our own uniformity."

Centuries after finally getting over racism, humans had mixed and matched in breeding so much that there was almost a uniformity to them as well, but like Kirby there were still those that tended to retain more of their ancient cultural identity here and there. There were also still some holdouts, or puritans, that had settled into isolated regions in the name of racial identity, but for the most part humans had grown past all the pettiness of race. Wyatt had often theorized that the experience of overcoming racism is what made humans so accepting of the alien races it had encountered. They simply refused to fall into the same judgmental traps that they had stepped into in the past.

The Samriza, on the other hand, had no history of racism in their species past. Or if they did, they had erased it completely from their history books. The Samurai all had identical skin tones and facial features. Even ancient manuscripts and paintings all showed them as looking the same as they currently did. It was as if they had all evolved along the same geographical line, or that was the only group that survived. It made it difficult in the beginning when they were forced to deal with humans on equal footing. The Samurai viewed themselves as superior racially and many still did. That view took a big hit, however, when the Samurai were forced to ask for help from the only other substantial space faring civilization, when they faced a threat from a spacefaring race known as the Manties.

The Manties were a large insectoid type species that operated on a hive mentality. In a nutshell, their point of view on life was that if something wasn't beneficial to the collective, it was eliminated. Other life forms were competition for resources and therefore must be destroyed. The first battles between the Samurai and the Manties did not go so well for the Samriza. The Manties were kicking the crap out of them, so a treaty of assured cooperation between the Samriza and the Human race was quickly established. Between the two, the Manty threat was eliminated and a whole new area of exploration and exploitation was opened up.

A few other species had been encountered over the years, the Reptica, the Claymen, and the Dooties, but none of them were as advanced or widespread as the Samurai/Samriza. Turns out, most of the time, the lights in the night sky, the abductions and the alien invaders, were us.

"We take great pleasure in our differences." Kirby nodded at, what he took as, a compliment. "But I'm sure anything is an improvement over Wyatt here."

"To say the least." Sonnet through in a she stepped forward. "Sonnet, Sonnet Melville."

Kirby took her hand in a very gentlemanly fashion, and bowed slightly toward it.

"Just call me Kirby." He replied. "It is a pleasure to meet you."

"So Kirby." Wyatt began, drawing his friend's attention back to the task at hand. "I don't know what kind of security or defense measures we're looking at here." He pointed at the ship to emphasize the possible dangers that messing with it entailed. "This was a pirate's ship, it has weapons that are beyond its class rating, and who knows what else is onboard."

"Basically, you're saying this could get me killed?" Kirby replied in mock surprise. "I appreciate the concern Wyatt, but I did a lot of research on this Zakicowi character and his ship. I know what I'm stepping into here. At least as far as my work goes." He then paused a thought for a moment. "You'll want your standard ownership package, I suppose?"

"To start." Wyatt replied, which earned him quizzical looks from his partners. "After I've gotten a chance to see what mods have been done I'll be able to tell you more."

Kirby nodded and set down his tool bag.

"Then I guess I better get started." He grinned and got to work.

CHAPTER 7

It took the better part of two hours for Kirby to finally bypass all the security and defense measures that the previous owner had in place.

"What did you mean, when you asked about the standard ownership package?" Sonnet asked as the door finally slid open.

"When a ship like this changes hands," Kirby explained. "There is a lot more to it than just handing over the keys. There are command codes, control configurations, and modifications to consider. A new owner will have to make certain changes in order for it to become his ship. Everything from the transponder code to the weapons on this bird are going to have to be changed in order for it to be legal for flight again."

"Does that take long?" Sonnet was nervous now, about how long they might be stuck on planet. She was anxious to get this expedition going.

"Usually only a couple of hours." Kirby shrugged. "This bird is going to take a little longer due to the weapons onboard, but not more than a day or so."

She relaxed visibly at that. She honestly didn't know why she was in such a hurry. There were still supplies to be gathered, hired hands to be brought in, and a myriad of other things to do. They didn't even have a destination as of yet, and still she was eager for the ship to be prepped. In fact, they all hadn't even determined if they were going to take this ship or Wyatt's other one. She then made a mental note to relax and exercise more patience. Still there was something exciting about getting aboard an honest to god, pirate ship.

The automatic lights on board came on as the airlock slid upward. The group then peered inside, nervous as to the next step. Kirby went up the ramp first. Slowly and cautiously. He was looking for anything that might activate a defense measure. A pressure plate, trip wire or bio signature sniffer, anything that might prove to be a danger.

"You finding anything?" Wyatt asked, as he drew his blaster.

"No." Kirby replied in a confused manner. "And that's what's troubling me."

Kirby suddenly found himself dodging a blaster bolt that had been fired at him from somewhere up ahead. It sizzled past his midsection, close enough that he could feel the heat as it shot by. He then dove down the ramp and out of the ship.

"Well I guess that's why he didn't activate the ships static alarm system." Kirby panted. "There is someone in there guarding the ship."

"Did you get a look at them?" Wyatt asked as he craned his neck into the ship to look around.

"I was a little busy, avoiding being shot." Kirby snapped back.

Wyatt forced himself to remember, that despite his time in the service, Kirby wasn't the combat hardened veteran that he himself was. Kirby had been an engineer and learned the trade of working on spacefaring vessels. It was true that he had been nominally qualified with small arms to repel boarders, and had been in combat, but fighting ship to ship was different than fighting person to person. Kirby had never even drawn his weapon from its holster in all his years in the military.

Wyatt crept up the entry ramp and looked quickly to his left and right. He didn't know enough about the layout of the ship to know whether or not someone could circle around to shoot him from behind. He also didn't know how many people might be onboard.

As he entered the hallway, he was surprised to see Kenjay had joined him, his own blaster retrieved from a holster Wyatt hadn't even known he was wearing. He was guessing, though, that swords probably didn't make good range weapons. He did note, however, that the alien did not look comfortable with the blaster. It was obviously not something that he had trained with as much as he trained with his blade.

Wyatt just caught the glint of a weapon being aimed around a corner at them and threw Kenjay to the ground an instant before the fired bolt smashed into the bulkhead directly behind him. Wyatt returned fire with two wild shots, more designed to keep his adversary from aiming properly than it was intended to kill anyone.

"Thank you, Wyatt." Kenjay sighed as he cautiously got back to his feet. "That might have been unpleasant." He then turned his head to glance at the still smoldering bulkhead.

"Just don't want to have to clean blood off my new ship." Wyatt huffed in reply.

The two then slowly picked their way forward. Catching glimpses of shadow here and there, up ahead of them. The long narrow corridor was not a place that Wyatt felt comfortable with when pursuing an opponent that knew the territory better than he did. There was nowhere to hide or even get under decent cover, should the shooter become ambitious in their attack. Of course, the reverse was also true, that the gunman would have to reveal themselves almost out in the open, for him to shoot at his pursuers.

Finally, the two explorers made it to an opening. It appeared that this hallway ended at a common area, that was probably at one time a dining hall. As Wyatt peeked in he could see where tables had been shoved over to one side of the room and turned on their sides. It would make good cover for someone to lay in wait. It would appear that this was the perfect place for an ambush.

Wyatt then pulled a black cylinder out of his pocket and turned toward Kenjay.

"Cover your ears and shield your eyes." Wyatt whispered to his alien partner as he slid a nose filter into his nostrils.

Kenjay was confused, but did as instructed. Wyatt then pressed the activating stud on the cylinder and tossed it into the mess hall. It sailed perfectly toward the overturned tables, bounced short, then hopped over to land neatly behind them. It was a textbook throw.

The loud boom from the sonic infiltration grenade, known on old Earth as a flash bang, would be deafening to anyone on that side of the room. The acrid smoke it spewed would then cause anyone in the vicinity of the device to choke and cough. The flash it emitted would also aid in blinding and disorienting any potential adversary.

Wyatt then charged, close on the heels of the distraction provided by his grenade, into the compartment. He ripped the heavy table out of the way, while dodging two wild shots from whoever was concealed there.

The shock on his face, when he threw the last bit of cover aside and saw a small, barely clothed, human female, shielding a Samriza child with her body. Still she swung her pistol to blindly fire at the threat that had just revealed them. Wyatt grabbed her arm at the wrist and deflected her aim, which caused her shot to smash harmlessly into the ceiling. She then, having identified the location of the threat she couldn't see, stabbed at him with a dagger concealed in her left hand.

Wyatt could see that there was no calming either the woman, or the child at this point, but he needed to gain control over the situation. He then brought the butt of his pistol down on the young woman's head, sending her into unconsciousness.

The child, still not being able to see, then leapt at where he believed the threat to be. He held short knives in each hand as he swung wildly, but blindly. Wyatt snatched the kid out of the air, slamming him hard enough onto the deck to drive the wind from him. From there it was easy enough to restrain him with binders Wyatt always carried with him.

"What do you make of this?" Wyatt asked Kenjay as he stepped back to catch his breath.

"I am uncertain." Kenjay replied. "But it does raise some interesting questions."

"Well I think we need answers." Wyatt huffed. "Let's see if this bucket has a medical bay, and if it does, let's get these two secured in it. I think they'll be safe enough there."

Kenjay nodded, and effortlessly picked up the secured boy and tossed him over his shoulder.

"You get the heavy one." He mused as he turned and walked toward the direction he believed the medical facilities to be.

"Let's just hope there is nobody else on board." Wyatt sighed as he picked up the young woman and likewise, tossed her over his shoulder. He did, however, keep his gun hand free, just in case.

After depositing the two combatants in the medical bay, Wyatt took a few moments to securely restrain them to the beds. The child had almost bitten him twice, and had succeeded in biting Kenjay at least once. But soon, the new owner and his business partner were once again making their way toward the bridge. Once there, they were able to use the ships interior scanners to determine the exact layout of the vessel and confirm that there was no one else on board.

"What do you make of our two trespassers? Wyatt inquired as he ran systems check after systems check. He could do most of the basic stuff, hull integrity, engine condition and a few other things, but he couldn't get into the more interesting systems until Kirby worked his magic.

"I think I shall reserve judgement until we have questioned them." Kenjay replied. "But the child does possess a resemblance to Zakicowi."

"That's what I was afraid of." Wyatt murmured.

"The vessel is still yours." Kenjay continued, giving Wyatt a curious look. "If that is what you are worried about. All of Zakicowi's possessions were forfeit to you when you killed him bringing him to justice. The boy has no claim, and as he is the son of a disgraced man, he has no clan."

That caught Wyatt short. *Certainly they don't punish the son for the sins of the father?* But as soon as he thought that, he knew it was true. There were cultures on old Earth that were the same way at one time.

"Well before we go down that road, let's get the facts from them." Wyatt then lifted his wrist computer. "Kirby. You got me?"

"I'm here." Came the sub-vocal reply, over the implants in Wyatt's brain.

"The ship is secure and ready for you." Wyatt informed him. "Time to work your magic and earn your pay."

"I'm on it." Came the chuckling reply.

"Now, let's go see what our prisoners have to say." Wyatt looked over at Kenjay, who nodded in response.

CHAPTER 8

Wyatt and Kenjay met up with Miss Melville as they headed down toward medical. It was not an area of the ship that left one impressed. It was evident that Zakicowi had put more emphasis on not getting injured, than what to do if he had been. That said some interesting things about his ship's potential.

Still the ill equipped medical bay was clean, probably because of the cleaning robots that were tucked neatly into their storage areas. It was also equipped with numerous beds that now had two persons strapped to them. The groggy female made no attempt to free herself, while the young Samriza pulled and strained at his bindings.

When Wyatt approached the young one, he actually snapped at him with his teeth in a vain attempt to bite him.

"Cease your struggle, young one." Kenjay ordered, only to be ignored.

"I'll not listen to one who had teamed up with a hairless standing dog!" The boy yelled back.

Kenjay looked over at Wyatt, who merely shrugged. As far as insults went, he had heard a lot worse. Kenjay, however, wasn't having it, and backhanded the boy hard and quick. The boy was stunned for several seconds after that. Evidently, he didn't get treated that way onboard this ship very often.

"State your name and class." Kenjay instructed the boy, feigning no more interest than he would have had in a cockroach.

"I am Oso Zakicowi. Son of Tishora Zakicowi" The boy grumbled. "Of the Zakicowi clan. First among Star-Reachers."

It was true, that the Zakicowi family had been the first family to set foot on another planet, at least among their people. They had a long and honorable history as travelers, explorers and conquerors. That was, until the family honor was blotted by the actions of Tishora Zakicowi. Still, by not acknowledging Zakicowi as a clan member, they had shielded themselves from too much stain upon their house. This action, however, would make sure that the boy would never be acknowledged by any clan member as a relative. It therefore, stripped him of all rights as a citizen. If Tishora Zakicowi couldn't or wouldn't be claimed as a clan member than any extension of him couldn't be either.

"As the son of Tishora Zakicowi, I claim rightful ownership of this vessel." Oso yelled. "I demand that you release me and my slave, and get off my ship!"

Kenjay smacked the kid again, only harder this time. He wasn't having any of the boy's insolence.

"You will remain quiet and respectful." Kenjay replied, calmly but forcefully. "You are non-housed. Denied by your clan. You have nothing, and claim nothing. You will remain silent until addressed, or so help me I'll eject you into space."

The kid's eyes went wide with surprise. Whether it was shock at the revelation that his father and therefore him, had been stripped of all honor, or the threat of Kenjay, Wyatt couldn't say. But it was clear that the boy believed himself to be more important than he was. It was also evident that he had not been completely educated about his own kind, however, as Master Kenjay's standing demanded more respect than was being shown. It was clear that the young one did not recognize Kenjay's ceremonial outfit or class ranking. Something that should have been part of his base training. It said disdainful things about his father, that his son should be so lacking in traditional education.

"Did he just say 'slave'?" Sonnet asked in a shocked voice.

It suddenly occurred to Wyatt and Kenjay that he had. The woman must have been Zakicowi's slave. Slavery was technically illegal in every quadrant, but had been practiced by the Samurai until it's treaty with the human race. Humans refused any dealings with a race that still practiced slavery and made the Samrazi outlaw it in exchange for help during the Manty war. Slavery of humans was especially heinous and was punishable by death in most instances. The problem was that there were so many outlaying systems that were basically lawless that even slavery was sometimes prevalent.

"It would appear that Zakicowi was a slaver as well as a pirate." Kenjay muttered. "His clan should be ashamed indeed."

Wyatt thought about the girl restrained to the bed and gave her a soft look. He had a soft spot for slaves, abused children and women in general, and she just about fit all three. He had fought against slavers while in the service, and had freed many caught in bondage. Many of those were children. The girl he now had restrained was young, although how young he couldn't say. When the human race could live to three-hundred plus years, it was hard to estimate age most times. Still, if she was over twenty s-years he'd be surprised.

"What is your name?" Wyatt asked her gently.

"I have no name." She replied, genuinely confused as to her predicament. "I was simply addressed as slave or number 4."

"Number 4?" Sonnet repeated as a question.

"My father was number 1, my mother was number 2, and my brother was number 3." She replied, as if the answer was obvious. "Zakicowi lost them in a game of chance. I was the only one left."

Wyatt looked at Kenjay and Melville and motioned them to come close.

"We need to let the authorities know about her." Wyatt whispered. "She's going to need treatment." Wyatt didn't want to say what kind of treatment, or at least he didn't want to admit it to himself. She had probably been abused, both mentally and physically. He would also wager that she experienced several rapes at the hands of Zakicowi. It only made him hate the alien even more, and actually made him glad that he had killed him.

"We cannot." Kenjay objected. "She may have information vital to our quest."

Wyatt's blood boiled at the suggestion. She was obviously of no value to Kenjay except at a parrot to whisper in his ear what she had heard.

"I agree with Master Kenjay." Sonnet voiced, surprising Wyatt. "Not for the reasons that he has issued, although she probably does have some information. No, I think we should keep her onboard and let her readjust gradually. Ripping her out of the only home she has known for so long would be detrimental to her physiological well-being."

"And you know this how?" Wyatt inquired, with a suspicious eyebrow raised.

"I'm a certified and licensed counselor." She replied, almost as if she was offended that he didn't know. "I specialize in trauma victims. I know what I'm talking about."

Wyatt searched his memory, and had to confess he had come across her degrees when he was researching her. Psychology was indeed one of her multiple doctorates. It was then that a little alarm bell went off in Wyatt's brain. He couldn't pin down exactly what was bothering him, but he was put on alert by something.

"I'll defer to your expertise in this matter." Wyatt finally agreed. Not that he liked it much. But if easing her out of the ship was the best thing for her, then by all means it was what was going to happen. "So what about our other passenger?"

"We could simply throw the spawn of Zakicowi off the ship and be done with him." Kenjay proposed.

Wyatt gave Kenjay a glare that would have peeled paint, but Kenjay simply shrugged.

"He is without honor or clan." The alien explained. "Therefore, he technically doesn't exist."

"We'll keep the boy with us." Wyatt announced, surprising his cohorts. "Where you, Master Kenjay, will educate him and train him." Kenjay started to object, but Wyatt held up his hand, silencing him. "Consider it a condition of my cooperation in this little venture."

Kenjay looked as though he was going to explode for a brief moment, but then he calmed, shrugged and nodded.

"A fair agreement." He mumbled after a moment of reflection.

"As for Number 4, we'll ask her what she wants to do." He looked sharply at Sonnet. "You will educate her as to her options and let her decide. If she agrees, we'll take her with as well. But she'll get a minor percentage. I think three percent sounds fair."

Miss Melville and Kenjay looked at each other and nodded slowly. They hated frittering away any more of the potential profits than they had too, but losing three percent would be inconsequential when the totals were calculated. At least if it all worked out in the end.

"Until then, I would suggest that we find better accommodations for our guests than strapped to these hospital beds." Wyatt finally grumped. "Let's see if this tub has some secure quarters we can house these two in."

CHAPTER 9

Kenjay and Wyatt paced the deck like a couple of expectant fathers, waiting for Sonnet to finish up with interviewing Number 4. It was then that Kirby came strolling up.

"Still in there eh?" Kirby observed with a smile on his face. "Well you'll be happy to know the ship is ready."

"So soon?" Wyatt was surprised. He was expecting a few days at the least. Not a mere twenty-four-hours.

"I transferred a copy of your AI to the mainframe and overwrote all of the old codes. I also put on a step-down transformer on all of the energy weapons to make them legal." He then leaned in close to Wyatt. "I installed the...*usual*...safeguards." He then gave Wyatt a look that said there was more to that story, but Kenjay was left in the dark as to what they meant. "All power rods are fully charged as well, and hull integrity is at ninety-nine percent.

"I also hacked the cargo manifest, and if it's accurate, you've got an impressive array of equipment in the hold." Kirby handed Wyatt a separate file chip that had the cargo listings on it.

"Such as?" Wyatt gave him the eye.

"Such as hover bikes, Jeeps, a heavy lifting crane, and even two construction pods that are configured for both atmospheric and space operation." Kirby filled him in. "There is some other stuff two, but those are the big-ticket items."

"Thank you very much. That sounds like we'll have an interesting time going through it all." Wyatt praised as he signed Kirby's digital order sheet to transfer the necessary funds. "If you're up for it, I'll have another job for you soon. Just stay by a com and I'll contact you. You've already got the codes for the *Stallion* should you need her." Wyatt reminded him, referring to the ship he normally piloted.

"So you've made the decision to take the *Revenge* on this little junket?" Kirby asked, almost knowing the answer.

"Yep." Wyatt replied, casually. "She's bigger, longer legged, and might have some clues as to what we're after hidden on board. Plus, its home to the two stragglers we've picked up and I can't see dislocating them just yet."

"I understand." Kirby then thought for a second. "You want me to call the cleaners?" Kirby was referring to a group of people that would 'depersonalize' the ship and remove all of the previous captain's belongings, they would also bio-clean the ship, making her feel like new.

"Not just yet." Wyatt grimaced, as it was something he would really prefer to have done. "We still need to go through her with a fine-toothed comb to make sure we haven't missed any secrets the old girl might be hiding."

"Gotcha." Kirby understood, at least as much as he needed too anyway. "Well, you've got my com address if you need me." With that he gave a wave and headed out.

Seconds after Kirby's departure the door to the quarters that Sonnet and Number 4 had been using for a debriefing and counseling session slid open.

Wyatt could see past the exiting Sonnet, into the quarters and saw Number 4, knees to chest, sitting on the floor, rocking back and forth. She didn't look like she had been crying, she simply looked, stunned.

"How fares our little one?" Kenjay asked as Sonnet wiped some sweat from her brow.

"To use a clinical term." Miss Melville began. "She's messed up."

Wyatt and Kenjay couldn't help but look at each other in surprise at her 'diagnosis.'

"She's suffering from PTSD from all the abuse she endured, and still in the back of her mind, believes that it's not over. That either her former master is going to return, or one of us, namely Kenjay, is going to pick up right where he left off."

"I gather it is because Kenjay and Zakicowi are both Samurai?" Wyatt assumed correctly.

"She simply can't differentiate between the two. At least not at the moment." Sonnet explained, to which Kenjay nodded. "It will come in time. Right now, she's terrified that if she doesn't keep watching out for Oso, she will be severely punished by either Kenjay or when Zakicowi returns."

"I had a feeling she was acting as his guardian." Wyatt rubbed his chin as he spoke. "Hence all the shooting at us."

"Guardian, nursemaid, playmate or plaything." Sonnet shrugged. "Any and all of the above. She was literally raising the boy so Zakicowi wouldn't have too. That's why he knows so little about his own culture. Despite it all, she feels a deep affection and connection to the boy. Something far more than Stockholm Syndrome. She is the closest thing the boy has to a mother, sister, whatever."

"So separating her from the boy would not only be impossible in such close quarters, it would be, what is clinically referred to, as a bad thing?" Wyatt inquired, latching onto her fast and loose diagnosis and running with it.

Sonnet simply nodded in reply. Thus, destroying any remaining arguments for removing her from the expedition. Secretly she was delighted as she was certain that Number 4, knew some of the secrets that Zakicowi would have kept aboard.

"Did you happen to find out her real name?" Kenjay asked, breaking his silence. "She was certainly not referred to as Number 4 by her parents."

"If she knows it, she didn't give it to me." Sonnet confessed. "She said that her mother referred to her as 'Dear One' and her father called her 'Child'. She hasn't seen any of her family in years. Near as she can figure, she's about twenty years old now."

"They were afraid to countermand Tishora's given title." Kenjay huffed. "They must have been his property for a long time. Or at least someone else's that deprived them of their cultural address."

It was at that moment that the door slid open and out stepped Number 4. Wyatt took a good look at her for the first time. She was tiny, no more than four and half feet tall, her long black hair was matted and ratty looking, and her eyes were a dark brown. She wore little more than rags, that somehow managed to cover her body. She possessed an ample bosom despite her obvious malnourishment, which was probably why Zakicowi had kept her when he lost the rest of her family. Attraction to certain areas of the female anatomy translated across several species.

"I must get to my chores." She stated flatly, as she tried to pass them all without looking at them. Especially Kenjay.

"Number 4." Wyatt called to her, firmly but gently. "I need to speak to you."

She stopped and turned to face the man, who for all intents and purposes, was her new owner.

"First of all," Wyatt began in a clear voice. "You must understand that you are free. That you are no longer a slave, and no longer property."

Sonnet gave him a warning glance, but he continued.

"So you have the option to remain with us, or to leave." Wyatt kept on. "We believe that it is in your best interest to stay. To let us to help you adjust. But we will respect any decision to leave that you make."

She looked at him blankly for a moment, meeting his eyes for the first time. She was obviously confused, but whether that was because she didn't understand or didn't know what to do, nobody could say.

"Where would I go?" She finally was able to squeak out.

"There are places that specialize in treating people who have been…treated the way you have been." Sonnet explained. "We would arrange for you to get treatment."

"Who would do my chores?" She sputtered. "Who would care for Oso?"

"For the moment, Master Kenjay has been honored with that duty." Wyatt smirked just a little at his alien business partner. "As for your chores, I think we can manage to pick up without you."

"This is home." She finally said softly. "I want to stay home."

Wyatt nodded slowly, realizing what Sonnet had said earlier was true. It would be better for her to remain and adjust slowly. Still, his own conscience demanded that he give her the option. He was not a slaver, nor would he ever pretend to be her owner just to learn what she possibly knew.

"Then you can remain for now." Wyatt put his hand on her shoulder in a supportive way. She flinched slightly, not being used to a touch that didn't demand something of her. "I am now captain of this vessel. You are now crew, not property. Do you understand?"

"Yes." She said as firmly as she could, which wasn't very. "Now may I go do my chores?"

Wyatt sighed, realizing this was going to be a long road for her.

"Yes." He replied finally. "You may go do your chores."

With that she turned and disappeared down the corridor. Probably heading toward the mess deck. There was a lot to clean up after the battle she had been involved in.

Wyatt then turned to Sonnet with an angry look that wasn't really directed at her.

"I want you to do what you can with her, as fast as you can." Wyatt grumbled. "I don't care how much time you have to dedicate to her. I want her functional, understanding what's going on, and I want her clothed in something more appropriate. She looks like a refugee, and I'll not have my crew looking like...like..."

"Slaves." Kenjay put in, finishing Wyatt's disconnected thought for him.

"Exactly." Wyatt shot him a hot look, but agreed. He then turned and stormed off toward the cargo hold.

"What was all that about?" Miss Melville, mused out loud, in the direction of Kenjay.

"It would appear that our good Captain has had some disagreeable experiences with slavers and their ilk." Kenjay replied calmly. "Whether that was from his time in the military or his time as a bounty hunter is more than I can say."

"What do you know about his career?" Sonnet inquired, knowing full well that Kenjay had researched Wyatt just as she had. She was also aware that he had many more resources than she did.

"I know enough." He said simply. At that he simply turned and walked back to the cabin he was sharing with Oso and disappeared inside.

CHAPTER 10

The next morning would be the next time anyone would see Wyatt. But the noise he was making was enough to make sure that everyone knew exactly where he was, and that he was very busy.

The previous evening, when he had stormed off, he had spent most of his time in the cargo hold, going through crates, boxes and looking over the materials stored in there. He checked the conditions of everything, done an inventory and then made arrangements for some of the cargo to disappear. In fact, that was what he was doing at the moment. As one of the construction pods, floated by, assisted by gravity unit, toward an awaiting transport.

"What are you doing?" Sonnet shouted to be heard over the activity in the hold.

"I'm paying my debts." Wyatt snapped back, somewhat harsher than he intended. He supposed the lack of sleep was making him grumpy, but he really didn't care. The others would simply have to deal with it. "Kirby requested one of the pods, in lieu of payment. Seemed like a good deal to me."

"That pod has got to be worth four times what his services cost." Sonnet grumped, watching more potential profit slipping away.

"What I do with my ship's cargo is my business." Wyatt grumped back in reply. "This will buy me some favors down the road. This business of mine is one where you can't have too much good will thrown your way."

Sonnet didn't like it. She still, in the back of her mind, believed that everything he had was subject to their partnership, which she knew was illogical. Still, the construction pod could have proved useful during any salvage operations. That was, if they ever got off the ground and on their way.

That was actually one of the many things she wanted to talk to him about this particular morning.

"I wanted to talk to you about crew, provisions and equipment we might need." Sonnet changed the subject to something she had more control over. "I have a few guys in mind for the expedition and I'd like to take Annwyl shopping with me."

"Who the hell is Annwyl?" Wyatt yelled back, to be heard over the work being done.

"That's the name Kenjay has given to Number 4." She explained. "He said it means Dear One, in his native tongue. One of the names her parents used to call her."

Wyatt considered the name for a moment and decided he liked it. Not only did it make perfect sense, it was pretty. Hopefully she would take to it.

"I have no objections." Wyatt finally replied. "It might do her some good to get out into the world. She probably hasn't left the confines of the ship much."

"She hasn't." Sonnet confirmed. "The only time she was let out was when they were in the middle of nowhere, and even then, she was required to wear a shock collar."

Anger flashed through Wyatt's mind as he envisioned that poor girl being shocked for some minor indiscretion. Again, he regretted the merciful and mostly painless way he had disposed of Tishora Zakicowi.

"Well hurry back from your outing." Wyatt finally replied, his mind wandering. "We still need to go over this ship together. We need to find every clue we can about where Zakicowi hid the *Rose*. As much as I respect Copernicus' ability and research, the fact of the matter it that it is entirely possible that this operation got him killed." Wyatt knew that kind of revelation wasn't what Sonnet wanted to hear, but he was going to speak plain. "And if his research got him killed, I don't see it doing us a whole lot of good in the long run. Finding the *Rose*, only to die of deep space respiratory failure doesn't sound like a success."

Sonnet, as she insisted Annwyl call her, made sure their first stop was a clothing shop. There she purchased the young woman, clothes, shoes, and a variety of self-care products. She then made their next stop the local physician and once she had a clean bill of health, they continued on toward the beauty salon. She wasn't going to go for runway model beautiful, but a good trim, washing and style might just make her feel more…human.

It was as they were leaving the hair dresser that things went terribly wrong.

"Miss Melville." An alien voice from behind them yelled. "I will have a word with you."

Sonnet and Annwyl turned to see three Samarzi standing in the middle of the walkway, heading their direction. Instinctively she drew her small blaster and stood ready.

The dart that hit her carried a small electrical charged that surged through her body like wildfire. The pain was intense and caused her to tense up spasmodically. She took a little comfort in the fact that her tensing up had caused her to squeeze the trigger of her blaster and send a shot toward the aliens set on confronting her. Whether or not she hit any of them was more than she could say. Still it was a thought that brought on the thought, that at least it would look to the world that she had gone down swinging, then her world faded to darkness.

"Where the hell is she?" Wyatt grumbled from the bridge of the *Revenge* where he and Kenjay had met up to start going over Zakicowi's files for clues to the whereabouts of the *Rose*. "Where the hell are they? I guess I should say. Although I wouldn't be all that quick to blame Annwyl for anything. I'm sure she would rather be back in her warm safe ship right about now."

"I believe you are correct about that." Kenjay agreed. "I sensed a certain trepidation from her, about her leaving."

Wyatt grunted in agreement, but decided to change the subject.

"So how are things progressing with Oso and his education?" Wyatt took a certain amount of satisfaction from the look of distaste that flashed across Kenjay's clay-like face.

"The boy is most stubborn." Kenjay admitted. "Also, I have put Annwyl's shock collar to good use."

A look of disgust and horror crossed Wyatt's face, but Kenjay held up a placating hand.

"I have only used it once." Kenjay assured the human. "And only to demonstrate my willingness to resort to it. It is not even powered up at the moment. I just wanted him to experience a bit of what he had been putting Number 4 through and see that he is not too good for similar treatment.

"After that little demonstration, his training and attitude began to improve. It will take more time than I am willing to dedicate to the boy, possibly even years, but he has shown the potential for intelligence, creativity, and intuition. He has also demonstrated that the one aspect of life where his education was not neglected, was combat. The boy is as good with a sword as any I have ever seen. At least for his age."

Wyatt nodded. It was saying a great deal, that if someone as established with a blade as Master Kenjay was, could be impressed with the boy, then he might not be a lost cause. Kenjay didn't get the title Master hung on him because of his family connections. He earned it the hard way. He was a sword master of the ninth degree, and there were only ten.

"Well I've got a feeling we need to learn everything we can about this ship and the Rose, right now." Wyatt grumped unhappily. "I believe it would be prudent to operate under the assumption that someone is going to be asking for all the information we've got here in short order."

Kenjay gave Wyatt a quizzical look, as if to ask how he knew such a thing, but decided that his partner's instincts were good enough for him.

The two spent the better part of three hours, going over the computer and reading all of the navigation files and pertinent records. There were some subtle hints here and there, but a lot of the trail one would need to follow had been deleted.

It was then that Wyatt took a renewed interest in the navigation table in the middle of the bridge.

"Something seems off about this table." Wyatt complained.

"It is a standard navigational projection table." Kenjay observed. "It can be used for everything from entertainment to course plotting. Three dimensional, holographic display and connected super memory. Your AI should be able to manifest interactively through it, should you desire it."

"I know all that, but something is bugging me about it." Wyatt then pointed to a small hole near the center of the table. "This, for instance. It's designed, not an accident. But why is it there?"

Kenjay didn't answer, but powered up the table to run a diagnostic on it.

"It would appear that there is a section of the table, and its files, that are not getting power." Kenjay manipulated some controls, but to no avail. "It must have a bad connection somewhere."

"Or a bad contact." Wyatt mumbled.

Kenjay gave Wyatt a confused look, but stared intently at him as he fumbled in his pockets.

"Where is that vial?" Wyatt mumbled absently. Then finding it, he pulled out the vial of mercury they had pulled off of Zakicowi's carcass. "I wonder…"

Wyatt then poured the fluid into the hole, noting that there was just enough to fill the void perfectly. The non-functional corner of the projections suddenly came to life, and a whole new set of accessible files suddenly appeared.

"Very good." Kenjay complimented him. He then sat down and stared at his native language. "This is in code, it will take some time to translate."

Wyatt nodded, grabbed a good, old-fashioned paper notebook, and started jotting down what Kenjay was translating. The two of them stayed that way until morning.

CHAPTER 11

"Captain!" Master Kenjay repeated louder than the previous three attempts to rouse Wyatt from his bed.

"What...what's going on." It took a few moments for Wyatt to realize where he was and why nothing looked familiar. He had been so tired when they finished working that the he decided to stay in Zakicowi's captain's cabin, instead of heading back over to the Stallion. He was not expecting much since pirates were not known for little things like cleanliness or personal hygiene, but he discovered that his quarters were immaculate. Probably due to the combination of Number 4 cleaning them and his small army of cleaning robots. Evidently Zakicowi was a bit of a neat freak. Fortunately, that philosophy seemed to carry over to his record keeping as well. The ship's inventory was accurate to the smallest item in the hold and candy bar in the galley.

"There is a priority message coming in over the com system." Kenjay explained. "It is addressed to you."

Wyatt rolled over and looked at the multifunction display next to his bunk.

"It's addressed to 'the hairless dog who killed the great Zakicowi." Wyatt grumped as he looked up from the message and gave Kenjay the evil eye.

"As I said, it is addressed to you." Kenjay shrugged, not bothering to defend the statement or Wyatt, for that matter.

Wyatt grumped a reply that wouldn't be fit to print and turned on his messages. In less than a second, the face of a Samriza that Wyatt thought he recognized, filled the screen.

"To the honor-less, hairless dog who killed Zakicowi, I present greetings." The alien began. He wore the traditional red armor, but had the rank of Master indicated on his sleeves. Except one of his armored arms was in a sling, blackened by a blaster bolt, and he looked to be holding it in pain. His clay-like face was unreadable, but his words were edged with fury or possibly pain. "I am Ship Master Curzo. Captain of the *Trudgen*. One time partner and ally of the great Zakicowi. As such I lay claim to his property.

"I realize that dog Kenjay, will try to convince you that I have no claim to his property, so I'll let, your friends convince you to turn it over to me."

The recording scanner swung over to reveal Sonnet and Annwyl tied up, with their arms stretched over their heads. Their toes barely touching the ground.

Wyatt sighed a heavy sigh as he looked at his two business partners and the predicament that they had landed in.

"Bring me Zakicowi's ship and personal effects. The coordinates are attached to this message." Curzo checked his wrist com. "You have two hours to comply." The screen then went black as the recording ended.

"Well there goes the morning." Wyatt grumbled.

"I assume then, that you are going after them?" Kenjay observed. "I would advise against it. It is most certainly a trap."

"Of course it's a trap." Wyatt barked back. He then paused for a moment, considering how to make Kenjay understand. "When you woke me this morning, how did you address me?"

"This is your ship. I addressed you as captain." Kenjay shrugged.

"So you've accepted me as leader, that is captain, for this expedition?" Wyatt inquired.

"Of course." Kenjay nodded. "I may not be of much use as a crew, but every expedition needs a clear chain of command. Your ship, your resources, your command."

"And a good captain doesn't leave his crew behind." Wyatt informed the now understanding alien. "No matter how annoying they are."

****

"Just relax Annwyl." Sonnet whispered to her charge. "We'll get out of this."

"If this is how you improve my life." Annwyl whispered back. "Take me back to the life of a slave."

Sonnet shot her a glare, but would have to admit that her taking care of her new friend, had not worked out the way she had hoped. It would be fair to say that her predictable life as a slave, might just be preferable to being kidnapped, and tied up by alien pirates.

The two were secured to beams running along the ceiling. They had been pulled up tight enough that it took effort not to hang from their restraints. Their wrists chaffed at their binders, and their arms and shoulders ached. Still, Sonnet tried to keep Annwyl's spirits up.

"Don't worry." She whispered with as much confidence as she could muster. "Wyatt will come for us."

"Your captain only cares about his new ship and any bounty he can lay his hands on." Annwyl spat. "He doesn't care about us. I'll even bet he intends on leaving us to increase his shares."

"It was his idea to cut you in on this expedition." Sonnet snapped back at the former slave. "He's the one that insisted you be dressed and fed decently. He's a better man than you give him credit for."

"He killed my master." She replied bitterly. "He'll kill anyone that gets in his way."

It suddenly occurred to Sonnet why Annwyl was so upset. Her life *was* predictable before. Yes, it was full of horrors, but they were the horrors she knew. It was stable, in its own crazy and abusive way. For the first time in her memory, her life was now unpredictable, uncertain and in no way, was it safe. Even with the abuse and rape she suffered under Zakicowi she knew he would keep her alive. She had value to him, even if it was only as one of his possessions. Wyatt had removed that anchor for her. Now she was unsure of her status or value. She had no understanding of what it would be like to be part of a crew or team that shared equally.

They had also taken away the only duty she liked, or even loved from her. She no longer looked after Oso. Perhaps that was a duty that they should return, even if only in limited fashion. It might also help Oso's adjustment if he suddenly had to deal with her as an equal, or superior instead of as a slave there to take care of him.

"Wyatt won't let us down Annwyl." Sonnet repeated, almost as much to reassure herself as her. "He needs us."

It wasn't much longer before the alien who had kidnapped them returned to check on them. He was an imposing figure, and the burnt armor he wore, with his arm now in a sling, did nothing to detract from his ability to frighten them.

"Your Captain has been informed as to our demands." Curzo gloated as he held his hand up to her face. "I'm sure he will attempt some foolish plan to try and rescue you."

Realization dawned in Sonnet's eyes.

"You want him to attack here!" She almost shouted in response to his taunting.

"Of course." Curzo laughed. "If he's attacking here, he isn't there. I knew there was no way he wouldn't try to betray me and fight to get you back. I would have probably won, but not without losing many of my crew and quite possibly myself in the battle. And in case you haven't noticed, I'm quite fond of myself.

"Oh there will be a welcoming committee when he gets here. A small one. Led by the miserable excuse for a man who caused you to shoot me. But they are expendable fodder, not full-fledged crew."

"Bastard!" Sonnet spat and threw herself at him out of anger.

"And then some, my dear." He laughed as he walked away. "And then some."

CHAPTER 12

Wyatt fired up the engines on the *Stallion* and made her ready for quick trip around the planet he would need to reach the coordinates Curzo gave him.

"Is not your other ship, better armed than this one?" Kenjay inquired as he buckled into the seat next to Wyatt.

"Better armed yes." Wyatt acknowledged. "Better suited for combat in atmosphere, no. The *Stallion* is designed to be just as nimble in atmosphere as she is in space. And I want every edge I can get against someone like Curzo."

"So you are familiar with him?" Kenjay continued, trying to somehow make himself useful.

"He took on the Riker's." Wyatt began. "A team of bounty hunters sent out to bring him to justice. A team of eight highly trained men. Only two of them are still breathing and one of them needs assistance just to do that."

Kenjay nodded, impressed and made uneasy at the same time. If Curzo could take on an entire team of highly trained killers, what chance did a lone gun like Wyatt have? Still, he had seen the gunslinger do some impressive things and his own research suggested that Wyatt was even better than he liked to let on, so he might as well trust the human.

"Where is Oso?" Wyatt suddenly changed the subject.

"He is secured in your brig." Kenjay replied, with a bit of a relieved sigh. It was obvious that he was already tired of playing teacher to the boy. "It is a most formidable set up you have there."

"I tend to get some unruly passengers." Wyatt mumbled in reply. Kenjay couldn't help but chuckle at that.

"Target coordinates aren't going to take us long to reach. Even with us on the other side of the planet, it's only going to be about twenty minutes." Wyatt informed his guest. "I'll be breaking the acceptable speed limit, and rattling some windows, but I'll get us there in short order."

Kenjay watched what he could see of the landscape, fall away and pass by under his feet at an alarming rate. He then felt his stomach lurch as the ship reached its apogee and started its descent.

"Al!" Wyatt called out to his AI autopilot/personal assistant. "Charge all weapons and ready defenses."

"Affirmative Captain?" Al replied, in a boorish voiced. "Shall I inquire as to our catch of the day?"

"Kidnapping rescue." Wyatt replied. "So minimal collateral damage on this one."

"Understood." Al replied, with a bit more enthusiasm.

Wyatt took the time to activate both defensive and navigational shielding. Defensive shielding was used to block and deflect weapons fire. Energy weapons, missiles and bullets were usually able to be redirected or defused depending on their power and approach vectors. It was much easier to deflect, or push away objects than it was to stop them completely. Navigational shields would brush away the constant stream of space debris or foreign objects a space craft routinely encountered while operating. The difference between the two were the power levels and the fact that defensive shields could operate on the ground, while navigational shielding could not. Also, navigational shields were limited in their dispersal of energy weapons. They did a fine job of protecting a ship from all kinds of radiation, but not when it was concentrated into a beam weapon.

"Missile alert!" Wyatt's AI copilot announced in calm, but insistent manner. "Two missiles on approach vector."

"Wow, they must really be determined if they are going to launch at this range, in atmosphere." Wyatt observed, dryly.

"The incoming shots are not ship fired, anti-ship missiles." The computer responded, much to Wyatt's surprise. "These are light anti-aircraft, shoulder fired, chemical rocket missiles."

"Those aren't even going to scratch my paint." Wyatt grumbled, a little confused.

"Speaking as the one who's paint it is," Al began. "I would still prefer that measures be taken to avoid impact. Which is in ten seconds."

Wyatt set his jamming system to its maximum setting and rolled the ship. He then put it on the best angle to both dodge the incoming missiles, and take minimal damage should they be struck.

"Why are they shooting at such a bad range?" Wyatt mused out loud as he watched the missiles miss and continue on harmlessly.

"I believe that they want you to know that they are there." Kenjay replied, looking a little green from the maneuvers they were completing. "They want your attention focused here and not elsewhere."

Wyatt thought about that for a moment then realization burst forth in his eyes.

"Al, are you still in communication with your twin?" Wyatt was referring to the copy that now existed in Zakicowi's old ship.

"Affirmative captain." Al replied, as if stating the obvious.

"Set all passive defenses to maximum." Wyatt commanded, alerting his AI that he believed an attack on that ship to be imminent and he was authorized to use lethal force to defend it. Normally, the defenses were in a passive mode and set to restrain and contain intruders. Lethal force could be used in passive mode, but only if any intruders got as far as the bridge. At the maximum setting, it was 'shoot to kill the moment they got onboard, and even before then, pressure plate activated stuns were authorized on the entry ramp.

"Settings achieved Captain." Al replied, calmly. "I'm having difficulty maintaining connection to my doppelganger. I suspect they are trying to employ a jamming device."

"Understood." Wyatt barked. "Don't divide your attention. I want you here for this incursion. We can deal with the other ship later."

"Understood." Al then fell silent as the AI's concentration was focused on the myriad of details involved in monitoring a ship going into combat.

"Why do you call your AI assistant Al?" Kenjay asked, mostly as a way to distract himself from Wyatt's piloting than any measure of curiosity.

"When I was a kid, I misread the identity plate for our home virtual assistant. I thought the A.I. was actually A.L. So, I started calling our home AI, Al." Wyatt explained as he turned on targeting computers and made sure weapons were hot. "So, I just naturally named my first A.I, Al and have ever since. The AI you are hearing is actually Al the fourth."

Kenjay nodded in understanding, and was slightly amused by the story of Wyatt as a youth. One never imagines a seasoned killer as a child.

"I'm getting sensor readings on the compound where the missiles originated." Wyatt's demeanor and tone seemed to change. He was making the transformation from Captain to warrior. From here on out he would be all business. No time for small talk. "Four structures, twelve heat signatures that match body heat. A mix of Samurai and Human." Wyatt then focused on the structure to the east. "Our hostages are right there."

"How can you tell?" Kenjay could distinguish no features from anyone of the signatures at this range.

"I'm not positive, but they are the only two humans close together." Wyatt explained. "It is more common for prisoners to be kept together than separated. Especially when the prison is improvised, like this appears to be."

"So it is an educated guess." Kenjay inquired.

"That's all life is." Wyatt replied almost too soft to hear.

Two more missiles were sent skyward as the *Stallion* approached the compound at breakneck speed. One actually managed to connect with the *Stallion*'s shields, but was exploded without causing any damage. Still the image of the weapons streaking toward the ship, frightened Kenjay to the point of questioning his willingness to be a part of the entire deal. But memory of the fact that he was basically bankrupt, helped put those doubts behind him. It was not as if he wasn't a skilled combatant, quite the opposite, but his area of warrior skill lay in the melee type of weaponry. The thought of seeing objects of death and destruction flying at him without him being able to do anything to defend himself, was unnerving.

Wyatt flew so low so fast that he had to use the takeoff thrusters and the landing thrusters to slow down enough to avoid crashing. Every passenger aboard sank down painfully in their seats as their momentum was arrested.

The two, missile-firing bad guys had the distinctly awful experience of finding themselves out in the open as the Stallion screamed to a halt, and were fried by the exhaust gasses being thrust downward. Wyatt doubted that there would be anything of them left to identify.

As soon as dust from the ship setting down was settled enough to see through, small arms fire began coming in from all directions. The gunmen swarmed forward as they assaulted the sturdy ship.

The main hatchway on the side of the ship slid upwards, exposing Wyatt in the doorway. Immediately a dozen shots, or more, came his way. He slumped to the deck of his ship in a slow, painful manner. The seven gunmen that had attacked, whooped and hollered in victory and stormed toward the now pilotless ship. It was not until they were almost upon the slain bounty hunter that the image that they were seeing flickered slightly and they realized they were looking at a clever hologram.

A large blaster suddenly slid down from a point of concealment in the ceiling, above the entry ramp and started picking off the exposed bad guys in quick fashion. Too stunned to move the villains attempted to return fire, with little success. Wyatt made short work of all of them from the safety of his bridge while working the semi-automatic weapon.

"Never expose yourself unless you have to." Wyatt said to Kenjay as he reviewed his scanners.

"That would seem to be sage advice." Kenjay observed, looking at the bodies of the dead henchmen laying around.

"You go check on the boy and make sure our little wild ride getting here didn't hurt him none." Wyatt ordered the alien. "I'm going to see to it, that Sonnet and Annwyl are safe."

Kenjay nodded and Wyatt disappeared off the bridge and out the ship. Kenjay only hoped that Wyatt had gotten all of the bad guys. It could get messy if he did not. He then remembered that Wyatt had said there were twelve heat signatures, two were his cohorts and nine had been eliminated. There was indeed, one left, somewhere.

Wyatt had made it to the area he believed the women were being held in short order. One more corner and he should be face to face with them. Carefully he edged a peek around to see if they were visible. From his position, he could clearly see Sonnet, but Annwyl was slightly behind her and not as visible. Not that it mattered as he could also see the man standing there, knife to Sonnet's throat, waiting for him.

It was the worst thing that could happen to him, with the worst possible outcomes.

"Come on out lawman." The man yelled out. His voice edged with fear. "I know you're there. Come on out where I can see you."

Wyatt stepped out slowly and carefully, as not to frighten the man.

"Go easy partner." Wyatt drawled. "Don't do anything feisty."

"It's about time!" Sonnet snapped as she laid eyes on Wyatt. "We've been here all night. Did you not notice we were missing?"

"Didn't rightly care." Wyatt shrugged. "Figured you could take care of yourself. Besides, if something happens to you, it's more salvage for me."

Sonnet shot him a glare, that by all rights, should have incinerated him on the spot.

"You two shut up!" The man snapped, pulling Sonnet's hair back for emphasis. "You drop your blaster Marshal. Drop it or I'll slice her." The man pressed the knife a little harder, making a tiny trickle of blood visible on her neck.

"Naw." Wyatt replied. "I'm not dropping my blaster. It's expensive and that's no way to treat a weapon."

The man looked genuinely confused at Wyatt's reply. It took him several seconds to process his reply and compose himself.

"Then put it down over there." He motioned to a table. "But do it quickly or she's dead."

"I'm still not really motivated to comply yet." Wyatt drawled. "Have you listened to her? She's a nag. Might just be better for me if you dispatched her for me."

Sonnet's look of shock was palpable, and the man's face wasn't far behind. He simply couldn't believe what he was hearing. Nothing was or had, gone according to plan and it was pissing him off.

"NOW YOU LOOK HERE!" The man shouted, pointing his knife at Wyatt in anger.

That was the break Wyatt was working toward. With the knife pressed so hard against her, shooting the man would have made him impale her. Now that was no longer a concern.

Wyatt drew his blaster and fired three shots as fast as he could pull the trigger. He scored direct hits on the man, sending him careening backwards. Silence then descended on the group like a hammer. Everyone could hear the man still sizzling from the hot energy that had burned through his chest and out his back. The air was rife with the acrid smell of blaster fire, burnt clothing and frying flesh.

Sonnet was in shock as Wyatt walked over to check the man. He was almost certain the man was dead, as he hadn't been wearing any ablative armor, but almost certain wasn't the same as absolutely certain, and Wyatt wanted there to be no doubt.

"I can't believe you just did that." Sonnet gasped. "Of all the irresponsible, jack ass moves you could have done. You decide to deliberately piss off a man with a knife to my throat."

Wyatt strode over to her quickly and held up a silencing finger.

"Are you hurt?" He demanded to know, to which she replied by shaking her head. "Are you alive?" Wyatt then asked with equal force. To which she nodded. "Then shut up, or I'll leave you up there until you calm down or all night if it strikes me."

Sonnet, considered a sharp retort, but fortunately for her she swallowed it. Instead she simply nodded and waited for him to find the keys to let her and Annwyl down. Wyatt still deliberately freed Annwyl first. Taking his time to let Sonnet down.

CHAPTER 13

The flight back to the dusty strip where Wyatt's other ship was parked was quiet, and uneventful. Sonnet was still seething and refused to come up to the bridge. Annwyl was sitting on the bridge, but quiet as always as she was still afraid of Wyatt. Kenjay was down in the brig, tending to some bumps and bruises Oso had obtained, but he would recover in short order.

"I expect I'm going to have to teach you how to fly." Wyatt drawled as he looked over at Annwyl. "Having a good copilot might just come in handy."

"If that is what you wish of me, mast…" She caught herself before she uttered the word that would probably upset Wyatt to no end. "Captain."

Wyatt did cringe a little as she caught the form of address that he had forbidden her to use. He would never be her owner. Captain, mentor, or friend, maybe, but never her owner.

"Al." Wyatt called out to seemingly empty air, which startled Annwyl. "Have you established contact with the *Revenge*?"

"Negative Captain." Al replied, with perhaps a hint of concern. "Either the jamming system is still active, or intruders have rendered the AI copy onboard inoperative.

There is also the possibility that the ship has been destroyed, or over written and stolen, or…"

"Enough Al." Wyatt snapped. "I got the picture."

"I never heard my master's AI speak." Annwyl suddenly voiced. It seemed it was her turn to startle Wyatt.

"I'm sure he had one." Wyatt replied. "He probably just had it on sub-vocal so he could hear it inside his own head."

Annwyl gave him a confused look. She had obviously never been educated as to the uses of modern communication technology. Zakicowi probably wanted to keep her as ignorant as possible. Especially when it came to shipboard technology she shouldn't have to deal with. He probably didn't want to risk her learning too much and then deciding to dispatch him and take the ship.

"You see," Wyatt began to explain. "There are these implants that can be put inside your head. They allow you to communicate with computers, AIs or other people, just by thinking about it. You think your words and they are transmitted. You receive them the same way.

"Then you can use a wrist com, much like the one I'm wearing, to interact with the web, watch entertainment vids or other things, right on the inside of your eye."

That thought disturbed her a little. The possibility of someone putting something in her eye was more than a little frightening.

"I'll set it up for you to have it done, if you like." Wyatt offered.

"Is there another way?" She asked.

"Oh yes." He replied with a smile, sensing her discomfort. "You can wear these plugs that go in your ears and contact lenses or glasses on your eyes and those will do most of the same functions. You won't be able to do sub-vocal, but the coms will still respond to verbal commands."

"So I would look like I was talking to myself?" She gave him a kind of wary look.

"Since the invention of the blue-tooth it has been impossible to tell who is speaking on a com-link and who is just crazy." Wyatt replied with a chuckle. "Don't worry. People are so used to it happening around them, that they don't give it a second thought anymore."

Wyatt's eyes narrowed as they approached the Air/Space port. His scanners were showing him some disturbing things. There were several people gathered around his ship, with several bodies on the ground around it. Evidently Al had been very busy defending the ship. It looked like he had gone beyond his programing if he had activated weapons that were firing outside of the ship. That said some interesting and disturbing things about the possible condition of the computer system. It was quite possible that Al's actions were the last act of a dying computer. AIs had, in the past, shown desperation and even fear when in danger of being erased or corrupted. It was entirely possible that Al had acted out of fear.

"I'm afraid that my other personality has gone and done something rather rash." Al offered as the screen images started to come through.

"Nice to know you'll go down swinging." Wyatt grumbled. "ATC isn't going to be happy about this though."

"I fail to see where Air Traffic Control is going to get involved." Al protested. "You are still a charged

Marshal. Even if you are not currently seeking any bounty. Defense of your ship, clearly falls under the defense of the law in this case."

Wyatt rubbed his chin and harrumphed in agreement. That would answer the question as to why Al thought he was justified in taking action outside of the ship. Wyatt was a peace officer and as such, his vessel was an extension of those duties, which included housing of prisoners. When the bad guys attacked the ship, they were essentially attacking a jail house. Law enforcement property, and as such lethal force was authorized. Wyatt only hoped that the local justice of the peace was as well schooled on the law as Al was. Or that he could be persuaded to agree.

Upon landing, Wyatt suffered a barrage of questions from the local authorities, but a combination of Wyatt's standing as a Bounty-Marshal and his good reputation put him in better stead than he would have anticipated. The locals were quite content with the elimination of several more disreputable members of their society and were very understanding about the manner of their demise as 'these things just happen.'

Old west justice. Wyatt thought as he walked away from his meeting with the local constable. *Got to love it.*

Kenjay and Oso were waiting for him as he boarded the *Queen's Revenge.*

"How bad is it?" Wyatt asked as he headed toward the bridge.

"I am not a ship handler myself." Kenjay began, most apologetically. "But I would say that it is not good."

Not good was an understatement, Wyatt realized as he stepped onto the bridge. Panels were torn out, wires hung from the ceiling and the navigation table was smashed. It was going to take a week to get everything back together, if he could find parts for it.

"I'm afraid your captain's cabin is not much better." Kenjay said softly. "I also regret to inform you, that your notebook has been taken."

"Well good luck with that." Wyatt grumped. "Between my own version of short hand, and my bad handwriting, they'll be a month figuring that thing out."

"My own memory as to what we deciphered is quite good." Kenjay announced with a smile. "However, my own ability to decipher the coordinates or other navigational clues is somewhat limited."

"Well write down what you can remember, and we'll try to reconstruct it." Wyatt sighed. "in the meantime, I've got to go talk to Kirby."

Wyatt turned out to be accurate in his assessment of the damage, as Kirby confirmed it would take him a week to make the necessary repairs. After Wyatt got done cussing a complaining about it, and the cost, he agreed to Kirby's recommendations and the mechanic got to work.

"Well this is going to put a crimp in our plans." Wyatt grumbled to Kenjay and Sonnet, who happened to be there when he was discussing things with Kirby.

"We also have the added problem that our time has become, somewhat, critical." Kenjay added. "Certainly, Curzo has much of the same information we have. It has become a race to the wreck, as it were."

"Why can't we take your other ship?" Sonnet asked, not wanting to waste time and lose the wreck.

"It's too small." Wyatt replied. "The *Stallion* doesn't have the cargo hold capacity for the equipment we might need for the salvage operation. It barely has the crew cabin capability for us all and would never carry enough water or food for a large group. Even if I let people sleep in the cells it would be cramped."

"But we only need to find the *Rose* first. Then we can stake our claim, place a salvage buoy and come back for the ship later." She continued to protest.

"And you think pirates like Curzo are going to respect our claim?" Wyatt gave her an arched eyebrow as if to emphasize how ridiculous that sounded.

Sonnet turned a little red at the rebuke, whether in embarrassment or anger, Wyatt couldn't tell. Still he had a very valid point.

"I believe our captain to be correct." Kenjay added. "As much as it pains me to admit it, we are simply going to have to live with the delay. Curzo still must interpret the data and make his way toward the region of space where we believe the *Rose* is located. Between Wyatt's shorthand code and his atrocious handwriting, that is going to take quite some doing."

Wyatt gave Kenjay a look over the crack about his handwriting, but even he would have to admit that he wasn't the neatest with his script.

"There is also the fact that the *Revenge* is much better armed and prepared for space combat than the Stallion." Wyatt continued, getting the subject off of his bad scribbling. "Should we run into Cruzo, or someone else out there, that means to do us harm, we might just want the extra firepower along."

There was a point that no one could dispute. Once it got out, and it would, of what they were after, they could probably count on a follower or two trying to horn in on their prize. History was replete with examples of those on the same quest competing for the same goal. And the parties were not always nice about it. Claim jumping and murder for monetary gain were still common crimes on the frontier. It would seem a prudent strategy to look as intimidating as possible, and the *Queen's Revenge* was a very intimidating looking vessel indeed.

"Anyway," Wyatt began, regaining everyone's attention. "I suggest we meet for lunch in the galley and discuss how to make best use of our delay. I'll be with Kirby for a little while anyway so we might as well not waste the time."

Sonnet and Kenjay nodded in agreement and turned to go their separate ways as Wyatt returned to assist his mechanic friend.

CHAPTER 14

"I suggest we use this delay to get our crew together." Wyatt reiterated as he sat down with his makeshift crew, as they gathered around a table for lunch. "I understand that each of you have experts in salvage and recovery operations you wish to bring onboard. Since we have six crew cabins, most of them fairly large, I figure you each can bring on two people. At this point in the game I'm more concerned with staking our claim and assessment of the prize than I am about a full recovery of the cargo or ship. Better to grab and go than get ourselves killed trying to bring the whole thing back. If what you're telling me is accurate even just enough to fill the hold of the *Revenge* would be an immense profit."

"What, exactly, are our accommodations going to be onboard?" Sonnet asked. "I've never been more than a passenger onboard a space liner before."

"I'll take the captain's cabin." Wyatt began to lay out what he thought was the best set up. "Master Kenjay will have a room to himself. You will have a cabin, of course. Oso already has his quarters and I see no reason to pull him from it, but if you would go through it and make sure he doesn't have any weapons hidden, I think we all would appreciate it." He gave Kenjay a look to which he nodded in reply. Oso gave Wyatt a sour look, but said nothing. "I also think Annwyl has earned a cabin of her own, but I expect the same precautions taken by you." Wyatt looked at Sonnet, and she nodded slowly in agreement.

"The last cabin is large enough and already has four beds in it." Wyatt finished up. "So your cohorts will have to pack light, but it's doable. We can also make arrangements for extra gear to be stored in the cargo bay."

Everyone but Annwyl murmured in agreement and all seemed satisfied with the arrangement. Sonnet wasn't thrilled that the two individuals she had in mind wouldn't have a space away from anyone Kenjay brought, but she didn't outright protest.

"Master...I mean Captain." Annwyl was quick to correct herself, and braced herself for punishment at her slip, but none was forthcoming. When no rebuke came, she continued. "I would like to share a room with Miss Sonnet." She asked, softly, immediately expecting her request to be denied.

Wyatt looked over at Sonnet, who shrugged slightly, then nodded.

"If that is what will make you most comfortable." Wyatt replied with as much reassurance as he could muster. "Then I believe it to be best. Her quarters are more than big enough for the both of you."

Sonnet was both a little frustrated and relieved. This would free up her people to act more independently, but would restrict her privacy, which was something she highly valued. Still, looking at the sad little waif of a girl, she couldn't help but give in to her request. There was also the thought that keeping her people and Kenjay's together might give her insight as to what he was planning. She didn't trust the alien, plain and simple. If forced, she would have admitted that some of that was prejudice against his kind, but more of it was his ruthless business reputation. She had calculated that he was planning a double cross somewhere, just as she had figured Wyatt to do the same, the trick was to be ready for it. In the end, she decided she would rather have her people by themselves than watching the aliens.

"Well now that sleeping arraignments have been settled," Wyatt continued the meeting. "I believe our next step is for you both to assemble your team. Also, there are still supplies that need to be acquired. I'll remain onboard to assist Kirby with repairs, while you two get the goods we'll need for this little junket. Remember that we're on a budget here, so don't go crazy."

Sonnet gave Wyatt a sour look at that, while Kenjay simply chuckled.

"An equitable distribution of labor, to be sure." Kenjay nodded in agreement. "I will have to purchase some supplies for myself and my comrades. Our dietary needs are similar, but not exactly the same as your own.

"As for my team, they only await my call. They were assembled the moment you agree to this little venture."

"What skills do they bring to our team?" Wyatt asked, a bit warily.

"Master Professor Awasa, is a brilliant geologist and physicist." Kenjay explained. "I have chosen him both for his ability to defend himself and his knowledge, in the event the ship is hidden in a cavern or unstable asteroid. He can also assist us with course projections and navigation.

"My second appointee is my personal pilot, Captain Taga. He can assist with piloting duties and any ship to ship unpleasantness we may encounter. He is highly rated in his ship to ship combat ability." Kenjay then stopped, cleared his throat, and continued on with a slight sense of embarrassment. "Just do not count on him for any hand to hand or close quarters weapon combat. His performance in those duties is less than exemplary. He is the type of person who is a genius in his narrow sphere, but rather pathetic outside of it."

Wyatt tried to look grumpy or disappointed at that remark, but his poker face failed him utterly. Instead he settled for just looking amused. He had seen people like Kenjay was describing often enough. He would even classify Kirby that way. When it came to ship repair and modification he was top notch, but put a blaster in his hand and he was just as likely to shoot himself in the foot as he was the enemy.

"What about you?" Wyatt suddenly turned to face Miss Melville. "Who are you bringing to this little shin-dig?"

"My first choice is Samtessa Green. A.K.A. Sam." Sonnet began. "I had not worked with her before, but she was top notch in her military class, rated pilot and gunner, and has degrees in alien archeology and geology. I was very impressed upon meeting her, and I think she will make a good addition in the cockpit and in any field work, we may encounter."

"And your other choice?" Wyatt prodded after a few moments of silence.

"Fox Pruit." She replied flatly.

"Fox Pruit." Wyatt repeated. "Not someone I would have chosen. How do you know him?"

"He worked for my father for several expeditions." She explained. "On this last trip, Pruit was already engaged in another contract. Which seemed to have been lucky on his part. Now that his other obligation has been cleared, he responded that he was willing to accompany me on this one."

"So who is this Mister Pruit?" Kenjay inquired, sensing he wasn't getting the whole story here.

"Fox Pruit used to be in my racket." Wyatt explained. "Got himself disbarred as a Marshal for taking a bounty off a non-extradition planet. That doesn't bother me none. Our kind is charged with bringing in guys when the real law can't go in. We deal with non-extradition planets all the time. At least the ones that don't mind you taking one more criminal out of their hair. The problem was, he smuggled out a very large man in a very small box. Still alive, I might add. The condition the man arrived in, convinced his superiors that he might not have the right temperament for law enforcement. So they used the violation of a non-extradition planet's sovereignty to fire him."

"And since then?" Kenjay pressed.

"Since then, he's mostly been a hired gun." Wyatt shrugged. "Working for whoever pays. Protection, extortion, security, you name it. Thing is, I've never heard of him betraying a contract or jumping ship for a better offer. Takes a job and sees it through. I can deal with that."

Kenjay nodded, noting the type of honor often found out in the west. A man's word was his bond. Many lived, and sometimes died for it. Simple, elegant, and often swift. It was the frontier way."

"So, is there anything else?" Wyatt looked at each person around the table in turn, indicating that it was a now or never time to speak. When no one voiced any other concerns, Wyatt nodded. "Alright. Let's get to it."

With that, everyone rose to leave. Annwyl at Sonnet's hip and Oso at Kenjay's.

CHAPTER 15

It took the week that Kirby promised, but they made good use of the time. Wyatt ran simulations for everything from docking to space combat, and generally familiarized himself with the controls and specs of his ship to the point where he could do emergency procedures in the dark, which sometimes happened.

Kenjay spent the time teaching and training both Annwyl and Oso in everything from history to swordplay. Oso was, at first, offended that he had to share his learning with a slave, but a few good strikes from Annwyl during sword practice, quickly disavowed him of that notion. She seemed to be overcoming her fear and developing a sense of vengeance. Kenjay only hoped she could put it in check and look past it or at least hold it in reserve until needed.

Sonnet also assisted in the teaching of the two youths. True, she leaned more toward Annwyl since she was her main focus, but she believed that keeping the two together as equals was helpful for each of their adjustments to their new reality.

Throughout the week the new members of the crew arrived and settled in. For the most part, this would give everyone the chance to meet and adjust before takeoff.

Finally, repairs were finished and final preparations were completed. It was getting to be time to pull up stakes and head for the stars. So, with people assigned quarters, introductions complete and supplies stowed it was time to leave on their adventure.

It had scarcely been an hour into the flight, and all the mundane departure routines, such as clearances, waiting for lanes to open and maneuvering out toward the hyper limit had been completed. That was when the bridge crew could finally relax and get ready to take the ship into hyperspace. For now, Al could pilot the ship, and guide it toward the jump point. Still, since this was the most congested area of space, a pilot had to remain at the controls. Not to mention this version of Al was a bit twitchy. Most likely because it was a new system, regardless of the reason, he hadn't earned Wyatt's trust yet.

"What is our course?" Fox Pruit asked as he strolled onto the bridge.

Wyatt in the pilot seat and Taga in the copilot position turned and eyed the man up and down in response. Fox was a tall man, with long dark hair that had started to grey at the temples. That grey worked its way down to the dark beard that hid his face. His eyes were brown, quick and sharp. There was a blaster, much like Wyatt's, hidden under the bullet resistant drover's coat he wore. His brown boots, with the pants tucked in, matched his brown gun belt. And he topped it off with a black hat, with goggles around the top of it. It was all very cowboy/steampunk, but he pulled it off nicely.

"You're not going to be one of those, 'are we there yet' passengers, are you?" Wyatt inquired with a bit of a grin.

"Naw." Fox replied in his usual drawl. "The longer it takes the more I get paid. So, I ain't in any particular hurry. Just wondering what to prepare for."

"Well our first stop is the Cassini Cluster." Wyatt answered, bringing a frown to Fox's face. "Tortuga."

"Not a real welcoming region." Fox voiced, with a bit of apprehension.

"That was the first breadcrumb." Wyatt replied. "Evidently Zakicowi had a stash out that way. Probably some kind of safehouse."

"Do you think they know we're coming?"

"Curzo has a good head start on us. That means I would side with caution and assume they will." Wyatt replied. "On the other hand, Curzo doesn't want any competition for the treasure, so he might just play it like Zakicowi is still alive. If any of Zakicowi's men find out he's dead, they may go looking to collect the riches for themselves. And some of them might have been with the pirate when he hid the ship, so they might know where it is."

"I thought Zakicowi killed his crew." Fox pointed out.

"That was the rumor." Wyatt confirmed. "But we already ran into his old first mate, and he was with two others. So the story about him killing his crew might just be a fiction designed to keep people from tying to hunt them all down. Might also just be a slight exaggeration as well. He may have only taken enough crewmen to help handle the ship and killed them when he hid it. That, I believe, is the most likely scenario, or else the first mate would have gone after it instead of gunning for me."

"Maybe he just needed a ship?" Fox offered. Which was an explanation that made a lot of sense. He might have known the location, but not had a way to get to it. It was worth considering.

"Thinking about this is making my head hurt." Wyatt rubbed the bridge of his nose as he felt the frustration of what they didn't know surfacing. "All this does is remind us that we don't have the information we should. We need answers, not more speculation. Mainly we need to know where Curzo is. And I have no idea how to find out."

"Well it might be a good thing that we're going to stop in Tortuga?" Fox asked, referring to the nickname of one of the most prolific pirate enclaves in the region. "I have some contacts there, I could send out some feelers."

A mental debate started to rage inside of Wyatt. On the one hand, having all the information on their most potential adversary might just make a lot of difference. On the other hand, the fewer people that knew about their mission the better. Wyatt was a big subscriber to the theory that 'loose lips sink ships.' And all that went with it.

"I'll have to discuss that with my fellow investors." Wyatt replied, not wanting to commit to an answer yet.

Fox simply gave a nod and tipped his hat as he left.

Wyatt watched him go and made sure the door slid shut behind him, before turning back to the controls.

"I get an uneasy feeling around that man." Taga offered as he too turned back toward the control console.

"Being that he's a hired killer," Wyatt mused. "I'd be suspicious if he didn't give you a case of the wiles. I suspect I do as well."

"Oh, you did when we first met." Taga explained. "But after Master Kenjay explained your aura, I relaxed considerably."

"My aura?" Wyatt chuckled.

"All living things have a degree of personality projection." Taga began. "To many this is read as an aura. A man that kills for a living, has a dark and foreboding aura. Yours is much that way, but occasionally your sense of honor, justice and compassion break through. These events, to many, would be read as bright flashes or vibrant colors that would soon get swallowed up again by the blackness. It is truly sad."

Sad? Wyatt thought, but chose to let the observation slide for the moment. He didn't need to be psychoanalyzed.

"How's Fox's aura?" Wyatt inquired. Curious about, if not believing everything Taga was saying.

"His is darkness that swirls in darkness." Taga replied. "It is almost as if he has accepted that this work is not only who he is, but how he will meet his end. He searches for something to care about, but acknowledges he will probably never find it."

"I think we all spend our lives much the same way." Wyatt observed. "Looking for something to care about, that is."

"We do indeed." Taga replied softly, then letting the cockpit fall into silence.

Taga then looked over the sensor information and saw something interesting.

"Captain," He called out in a more formal manner. "We seem to have picked up a sensor shadow."

Wyatt transferred the information he was looking at to the main screen and studied it carefully.

"Looks to be an echo." He mused. "Some kind of false image."

"Has this vessel indicated a tendency to do that?" The copilot inquired while making several different sensor adjustments.

"Haven't had this beast long enough to answer that one." Wyatt confessed. "It's keeping the exact same distance and speed. Be pretty hard to do that if it were another ship." Wyatt made some course adjustments, and then correct them. "It stays right there without any variance. I've only ever heard of sensor shadows doing that."

"I as well, have never experienced anything other than what you have described." Taga confirmed.

"Well, keep an eye on it." Wyatt ordered. "Even if it is only a shadow, it will be good to know the quirks of this ship."

"Aye captain." Taga agreed with his captain's assessment. Even if the shadow was harmless, it was always good to know one's ship. "Will do."

CHAPTER 16

The group did indeed like Fox's suggestion that they make for the pirate outpost of Tortuga. To say it was a pirate outpost was a bit of a misnomer, as the authorities would have certainly stormed in and taken any place that actively shielded pirates. That being said, it was an open secret that the place was crawling with them.

Oh, there was a time when the government sought to stamp out the piracy trade and bring law and order to the galaxy. They even made significant headway in cleaning up the place. Until several of the regional governors realized just how profitable piracy was. Shortly after that epiphany, the realization of just how profitable politics could be, soon followed. After the bribes started to flow, law and order were severely curtailed and extradition was banned. Now the government walked the fine line of letting the pirates do just enough to not attract the attention of the more powerful star systems and keeping the powerful star systems at arm's reach.

"Give me a course projection." Wyatt looked over at Taga, who immediately complied. "I need to know when we reach the closest point to the primary."

The point in question appeared on the screen, along with a dotted line that indicated their course.

"We will reach that point in twenty minutes." Taga informed him.

"That should be enough time." Wyatt mumbled. "Have the crew muster in the cargo hold."

"Aye sir."

Twenty minutes later the crew was gathered around a metal tube, in which was laid the body of one Tishora Zakicowi. The coffin had been sealed, as the shell had not been embalmed. But Wyatt had insisted that he at least be dressed in ceremonial robes, if not his armor.

"Ladies and gentlemen." Wyatt began, somewhat uncomfortably. "We are gathered here to commend to space, one Tishora Zakicowi. A being of space, he had spent most of his life between planets. I think it only fitting that out there is where he finds his final resting place."

Wyatt paused to give anyone else a chance to speak, but no one disagreed with him. Not even his son, who looked very sullen.

"Master Kenjay," Wyatt began. "I understand that your people have a custom of a poem to be recited for the deceased."

For a split second, Kenjay looked as if he was going to object. Then he looked down at the boy and softened. Ordinarily one without honor was not worthy of the reciting of the Master's prayer, but he would make an exception for the son of the dishonored brethren.

"When breath has left my humble body, may my spirit find solace in the great beyond. May my life have been one worthy of song, and my heart full of cherished thoughts of those I leave behind. I now go to soar with my ancestors, may I be carried on the winds of honor."

It was less than a prayer, but more than a statement. And it managed to bring a tear to both the lost boy and Sonnet. Even Annwyl, the one Zakicowi had abused and tormented, seemed to feel a bit of sadness at his passing, at least at the moment.

Wyatt then walked over to Oso and presented him with his father's sword.

"I'm giving you this because I believe it would be what your father would have wanted." He then looked at Kenjay. "But Master Kenjay will hold onto it until he believes you to be ready."

Oso nodded, but said nothing. A single tear, managed to break through his defenses and run down his cheek.

Then, Wyatt activated the airlock, and ejected the tube into space. At the speed they were traveling, it would take years for the coffin to reach the sun, but that seemed to be the most appropriate burial for the explorer, pirate and father.

Landing was pretty straight forward, even without the proper permits being on file. The assurance of a payout of a few credits was enough to put in a backdated request for landing. Something simply overlooked due to bureaucratic red tape, no doubt.

"Are we going to be safe here?" Sonnet asked, a little nervously. "I mean in Tortuga proper?"

"Not even remotely." Wyatt replied a little sourly. "Especially not for me."

"Why is that." She asked, her brow furrowing.

"I believe our good captain," Kenjay offered to explain. "Is pointing out that as a peace officer, he will not be very welcome here. In fact, I would highly recommend that you remove your star."

"Good idea." Wyatt nodded as he reached into his spun tritanium vest, and removed the magnetic badge. He then put on his ablative trench coat and got ready to depart the ship. "By the way, do you know if your man has arrived yet? Awasa, I believe you called him?"

"He has sent a communique that he will not be joining us." Kenjay admitted. "It would appear that he has contracted something that will prevent him from traveling. As he put it, he is most unwell."

"I see." Wyatt nodded. "Well better he stays put, than get the entire crew sick."

"I agree." Kenjay nodded. "I believe that our search might have been easier with him along, but I do not think that his will put that big a disruption in our plans."

"So where are we going?" Sonnet asked, apprehensively, changing the subject from non-present aliens. "I mean where to first?"

"Best place to find out information on pirates around here is a guy named Cornwall." Wyatt replied easily. "He's connected to both the government and the pirates, under the pretense that he his writing about them. Kind of a living historian thing. To be honest he does keep up a running blog that documents the activities of modern pirates and he manages a comparative history with pirates of old. All the names are changed, of course, and everything is passed off as fiction so that no one accuses him of being a spy or an informant, but he keeps his fingers in everyone's pie.

"Personally, I think he's just biding his time to take over the whole place, but that just might be my suspicious side talking."

"So where do we find this Cornwall?" Kenjay inquired.

"He's got a nice little bungalow just outside of town." Wyatt replied. "But the first place we want to look is the *Patched Parrot*. It's a saloon, just off the space port. Not a nice place, so mind your step."

"Couldn't make it sound any more pirate-ish?" Sonnet quipped, which earned a few chuckles.

"Believe it or not," Fox through in. "Tortuga has managed to gain a little fame in the underground tourism trade, by playing up the pirate image. So a lot of businesses go out of their way to play up the 'peg leg, parrot on the shoulder, eye patch' image. I suspect, that someday, when this region of space is more civilized, Tortuga will set up their own pirate theme park to cash in on the notoriety."

"I can see it now." Wyatt mused. "A bunch of scantily clad waifs and wenches, greeting the tourist, and busing them over to pirate ship shaped hotels and restaurants. Complete with casinos and buccaneer floor shows."

Sonnet couldn't tell just how sarcastic Wyatt was being, so she decided not to challenge his version of the future. For all she knew, he might just be correct.

"So what's the plan?" Sonnet finally asked, mostly to change the subject.

"Fox, Green, Kenjay and myself." Wyatt began. "Go down to the Parrot and start *poking* around. After that, if needed, we head over to Cornwall's bungalow.

"Somewhere along the way, I've also got to send a hyper-cable to Kirby to give him an update."

"You're telling him everything that's going on?" Sonnet gasped. "This is supposed to be secret."

"Hey!" Wyatt barked at her. "Kirby is our cavalry should anything go wrong. Not to mention, he's the closest thing I have, to local kinfolk. I trust him. More than I trust you." Wyatt gave her a glare that made her wilt.

"Anyway, someone has to stay here with Annwyl and Oso." Kenjay added in, taking some of the heat off Wyatt. "Wyatt has determined that you, with your counseling credentials, are the most qualified to remain with Annwyl and thereby Oso. Taga will also remain aboard to see to piloting duties and ship security, and will assist in watching out for the two young ones."

"Besides, Sonnet." Fox joined in. "Green, Wyatt, and myself are all experienced in the rough stuff that might ensue. I can't speak for Kenjay on that subject."

"Rest assured, Mister Pruit," Kenjay gave the gunslinger a bit of a wry look. "I did not earn my title as Sword Master by using my family connections." Something that Kenjay was ashamed to say, happened quite frequently, despite his race's emphasis on honor and hard work. Nepotism and politics was the same all over or so it would seem.

"Then it's settled." Wyatt finished, without waiting for more objections from Sonnet. "I suggest we get moving. We're burning daylight."

CHAPTER 17

It wasn't long before the four adventurers found themselves standing across the street from, and looking at, the *Patched Parrot*.

True to its name, the institution sported a several different renditions of a beautifully plumaged, multicolored, parrot, sporting an eyepatch and peg leg. The pirate theme didn't stop there either. The parking posts out front were made to look like a ship's rails, the windows were oversized portholes and the door was made to resemble a hatchway. Inside, the motif continued with life preservers on the wall, random ropes hung to resemble rigging, and dozens of pictures of ships from the very modern to the most ancient galleon. Skull and cross-bone flags hung in several places and other nautical themed attire was distributed about.

Not satisfied with the establishment looking like Long John Silver's living room, the employees, of which there were a half dozen, all wore costumes that looked like they came straight out of a Halloween shop. Every possible pirate stereotype was visible.

The few customers that were languishing about, did nothing to dispel the pirate persona either. They were dirty, heavily armed, and suffering from various levels of intoxication, despite the early afternoon hour.

"May I help you?" A man dressed in white, frilly shirt, black vest, striped pants, and a phony hook for a left hand inquired.

"I'm looking for Cornwall." Wyatt replied in a gruff, direct manner. He was in professional mode now. Taking in every angle he could and searching for every threat. He was determined not to make the same mistake he made at the *Plush Horse*, when he missed Kenjay standing in the shadows.

"One on the catwalk." Fox whispered to Wyatt as he too, searched for threats.

"Two by the kitchen." Green also threw in.

Green was still something of a mystery to Wyatt. He hadn't seen her much since she joined up with the company, but what he had seen had impressed him. She was brilliant, fearless and tough as nails. She had left a promising career in the marines to go back to school and learn about the things in the universe that fascinated her. Still she kept her dark hair worn as a crewcut and she preferred to wear clothes that looked like they came from military surplus. Her dark eyes were quick and intelligent and her body was in top notch condition. Half the time she had been onboard she had spent exercising in the cargo hold. She was attractive in a rugged sort of way and she had the attitude that she aware she wasn't going to be everybody's cup of tea, and that was something she didn't give a single solitary damn about.

"Marshall Wyatt Toranado!" Someone called out from across the room. "You've got a lot of nerve, showing your face here."

People scattered, and the man playing host was looking to make himself scarce as a very large, lumbering, and seemingly intoxicated Samrazi started making his way toward the group. Tables, chairs and other patrons flew to the side as the huge alien strode, unhindered toward the group.

Fox reached for his blaster, but Kenjay put his hand on his to stop him. Wyatt had made no move yet, so Kenjay stepped in front of his captain.

"I would advise against hostile actions against this human." Kenjay offered in a commanding voice. "You will find no easy prey here."

"Out of my way small ling." The alien boomed as he approached the much smaller sword master. "I'll have my words with the hairless dog, not you. But if you want to discuss your betrayal of the honor of your own kind by working with this filth, I'll save time for you after."

"You'll make time for me now." Kenjay roared as he drew his blade. The mysterious metal sang as it cleared its sheath and a smile of satisfaction crawled across his face.

"Kenjay." Wyatt whispered softly to the alien he regarded as a friend. "We need information. Just humiliate him, don't hurt him."

Kenjay gave a barely perceptible nod, but seemed to agree with Wyatt's viewpoint.

The large alien drew a blade of his own, but his was shorter, with more of a curve to it. More like a cutlass than Kenjay's Katana looking weapon. He then attempted to simply push Kenjay out of the way, only to have his hand slapped, painfully, by the sword master's blade. Kenjay had turned it, as not to cut the blustering alien's hand, but it still smarted.

"I see you need a lesson in minding your own business." The alien roared, as he turned to face Kenjay.

Blade met blade with a loud clang as thrust, parry and repost became the order of the day. Kenjay was honestly enjoying himself, as the endorphin rush of this kind of combat flowed through him. He outclassed his opponent and he knew it. It was just a matter of beating him, without hurting him. If Wyatt had not put on that little caveat he would have already dispatched his opponent.

The alien wasn't unskilled with his weapon, he was simply nowhere near the level of Kenjay. He would thrust, only to have his blade deflected or to discover his adversary had deftly moved to the side. The flat strikes he was painfully receiving, were letting him know that Kenjay could have sliced him up already if he wished. This frustrated him all the more, knowing that he was being toyed with.

Kenjay let the battle rage on, for several minutes before he decided he had enough exercise for one day. He then waited for the overhand strike the alien seemed to like and instead of blocking it, as he had done previously, he dodged to the side and let it embed itself in a table. He then brought his own blade down, snapping the cutlass in two.

The alien stumbled back in disbelief, still holding the useless hilt of his weapon. His left hand then reached down toward the blaster on his hip, only to have it shot away, by Wyatt's lightning fast and deadly accurate draw.

"That's enough you." Wyatt grumbled. "Now move, toward the back."

Everyone fanned out around Wyatt as he led the alien out the back of the establishment and out into the alleyway.

Once outside, Wyatt got in the alien's face with an intimidating look about him.

"Now it's time you get what you've got coming to you." Wyatt growled as the alien backed against the wall.

Wyatt stepped forward and surprised everyone by giving the enormous samurai a huge bear hug.

"Cornwall!" Wyatt shouted, earning confused looks from everyone around him. "Agnus Cornwall, how the hell are you?"

"I'm good Wyatt, but did you have to wreck my blaster like that? Those things are expensive." Agnus returned in a low, gravelly voice. "Anyway, it's good to see you."

"Would you mind explaining just what the hell is going on?" Kenjay demanded as he sheathed his blade. "I almost killed this brother."

"Agnus Cornwall, meet Master Kenjay." Wyatt introduced them to which they each bowed in the traditional manner and exchanged the traditional greeting. "Cornwall here is the person we're here to see. But we can't just walk up to him and start asking questions."

"I have a cover to maintain." Cornwall explained. "If the pirates, or government, think I'm giving information too freely, they'll stop talking to me. Maybe even kill me. But you still owe me for a new blaster, and cutlass." He gave a sharp look at Kenjay, but it lacked any real intensity.

"In order to talk to Cornwall here, we have to make it look like he's being coerced." Wyatt finished explaining to the group. "I'll transfer enough for some new toys. But only if the information is good."

Cornwall mumbled something in agreement, but still wasn't happy.

Kenjay nodded in understanding, but he too was still fuming. It would take time for his temper to subside, but he understood the logic and appreciated Cornwall's delicate position.

"You have an unusual name for one of our species." Kenjay pointed out, making it clear he was looking for the story there.

"I was found aboard a drifting freighter." Cornwall explained. "At the time relations between our people were strained and communication limited. The doctor, of the ship that found me, raised me for many years, until relatives were found and I was returned to our people. I took his name to honor him. He gave me a good life, when he didn't have to. That's also how I met Wyatt here. We were in school together. He came to my aid more than once, when less open-minded humans objected to my presence among them."

"I see." Kenjay nodded. His trust and honorable view of humans was raised another point. At least where Wyatt was concerned. Still the humans that were prejudiced against him were young and would probably grow out of their ignorance.

"So what can you tell us about Curzo and the *Western Rose*?" Wyatt pressed. Trying to get the conversation back on track. He knew that their time was limited.

"The *Western Rose*?" Cornwall repeated, before realization dawned in his eyes. "Oh yes. That Well Argo stage that got robbed."

People around him nodded as he made the connection.

"Well Curzo arrived here two days ago." Cornwall continued. "He was going on and on about finding the stage. He never called it by its name so it took me a moment to put the two together. But he kept saying he had a solid line on it, and needed some crew to help with salvage. Funny thing is, for a guy who was supposed to have all the answers, he spent a lot of time at the research library, nav center and communication hub."

"So he doesn't know." Wyatt concluded.

"I'm willing to wager he's still trying to put all the pieces together." Cornwall grinned. "I saw a bit of the star map he's got. It's not complete."

"So where can we find Zakicowi's old hideout?" Wyatt pressed.

"Ah the worst kept secret in Tortuga." Cornwall chuckled. "Zakicowi has a base on the far side of Samurai Moon. I'll com you the coordinates. If you're looking for answers, I'll bet that is where you'll find them. But beware, it is supposed to be heavily guarded. That is why none of the other pirate clans have tried to take it from him. Of course, as soon as they all find out he's dead, that's likely to change."

"Didn't Curzo tell them?" Wyatt gave him a suspicious look.

"No, he did not. The only reason I'm aware of it, is contacts in the government. The announcement came in on one of the criminal blotters. It was a minor mention, and not picked up on by very many people." Cornwall revealed. "Anyway, Curzo had claimed to have partnered with Zakicowi for the information. Probably to improve his standing in the clans. If Curzo and Zakicowi are a team, they would be pretty powerful and being the last two of the old clans, they would have plenty of experience between them. Not that many of the new clans are in a position to challenge Curzo in the first place, those are still getting established and trying to carve out their own little niche. Most of the old clans were wiped out when they took the *Rose* in the first place."

"So Curzo is hoping to ransack Samurai Moon and find out what Zakicowi has there." Wyatt rubbed his chin in thought. "Probably hopes to find any clues left behind."

"That's a safe bet." Cornwall agreed. "And I'm willing to bet that the answer are there, if he can find them."

"Any thoughts?" Wyatt raised an eyebrow in his longtime friend's direction.

"Well, Curzo is tenacious and fearless, and very direct, but he's not the most creative sort." Cornwall mused. "So he's probably going to be wasting a lot of time pounding on the front door."

"Which leaves us free, to go around the back." Wyatt finished for him.

The group then all got the same matching, hungry smiles.

Later they gathered back at the ship to fill Sonnet in on their findings. Even Cornwall walked back with them, although he insisted that his hands be bound. He still had to keep up appearances.

"We are going to Samurai Moon then?" Annwyl inquired. A bit of hopefulness in her eyes.

"Seems like the place to start." Wyatt replied. "Just let me make a quick stop at the com center and we'll meet back at the ship."

"We might need some more weaponry as well." Fox added. "Cornwall said the place was heavily guarded."

"It is not." Everyone stopped to look at Annwyl in disbelief.

"What was that?" Wyatt demanded.

"It is not heavily guarded." Annwyl explained. "Master went to great lengths to make people think that it was, but there was never anyone there other than Oso and myself."

"Well I'll be." Cornwall gasped. "If I had known that, I might have gone out there when I heard the news myself."

"Oh there are defenses." Annwyl was quick to clarify. "But they are mostly on automatic. There are traps as well."

"Oh." Cornwall seemed to deflate a little. Perhaps he was relieved that he had believed the stories about the place after all.

"Well, let's get moving." Wyatt announced. "Might as well not waste any more time then we have to."

"In that case I'll make myself scarce." Cornwall announced. "It was nice meeting you all, and I wish you luck."

He then gave Wyatt one more bearhug, lifting the smaller man from the deck. "You take care now." He warned with warm concern. "And try to visit more often."

"I will old friend." The two then parted and Wyatt got down to business.

CHAPTER 18

The moon, known as Samurai Moon, was not tied in orbit around any planet. The theory was that at one time it was within the gravity arch of one of the gas giants in the system, but broke away to wander through space as a lonely moon. That same tearing away did a lot of damage to the integrity of the body. The surface was badly scarred, raggedly cragged and it trailed debris and dust like an enormous comet. It was gradually heading toward the systems primary sun, but would be centuries getting close enough to become uninhabitable.

There was a time, when the moon was a hiding place and base of operations for several pirate fleets. But internal squabbling, the lack of physical stability and the inhospitable approaches to the lunar body, due to the drifting debris, had made it less than desirable to approach. This was probably what appealed to Zakicowi, who, unlike Curzo, was an imaginative sort and a highly skilled pilot.

The comparison between the two pirates couldn't have been starker. Zakicowi was the brains of the operation, the strategist and the one who favored finesse over brute strength. Curzo was the blunt instrument, the brute and the tactical genius. Together they fought like cats and dogs, but also made up the best team. It would be like teaming up Bartholomew (Black Bart) Roberts and Edward (Black Beard) Teach. Black Bart being the one that played the long game, read people perfectly and was an excellent seaman, despite his never having wanted to go to sea in the first place. Whereas Black Beard ran his own flagship aground twice, and relied on his reputation as a warrior bear to intimidate people into surrendering. A reputation he only earned when faced down in the end.

"Do we know what we are looking for?" Kenjay asked as they started getting good looks at the moon.

"Cornwall sent over some sensor readings as well as coordinates." Wyatt replied. "They aren't perfect, but we've got a good idea of where the base is located. Probably could have used the nav computer to fly us in unassisted if it hadn't been smashed by Curzo."

"What has the boy said about this place?" Taga asked of his master, from the copilot seat.

"He has been tight lipped about it." Kenjay sighed. "I have tried every negotiation tactic short of torture, but the boy will not reveal anything. I believe that he thinks that informing us about this place would be akin to him betraying his father's trust."

"He may not know anything either." Sonnet added. "Nothing we've seen out of him indicates that his father taught him anything other than how to fight."

A murmur of agreement washed around the bridge at that. Most people onboard had come into contact with Oso only briefly. But even that seemed to be enough. He was rude, crude, and overbearing. Despite his size, he was a fierce fighter and would take any opportunity to take offence and force a confrontation. Unfortunately for him, even though he was highly skilled, everyone else onboard, with the exceptions of Taga, Sonnet, and Annwyl, were professional fighters. And outclassed him in almost every way. Oso had received several bruises in response to comments made or challenges accepted. He was slowly learning respect, but it would be a long road.

"Where is he?" Wyatt asked, slightly looking around.

"He is currently in the guest quarters." Kenjay answered with a grin.

The guest quarters were a makeshift brig, made out of an old shipping container in the hold. Kenjay insisted on building it, citing that if the *Queen's Revenge* had any secrets or hidden ways to communicate off of the ship, they would probably be in Oso's quarters. The last thing they needed was someone tipping their hand as to their intentions or whereabouts.

"What about Annwyl?" Wyatt then asked Sonnet. "Is it possible that she knows anything?"

"She claims to be familiar with the layout of the place from the inside, and has drawn me a crude map, but she was always locked in her quarters for the approach, so she wouldn't be able to give away its location should he lose her in a poker game." Sonnet spat that last part. Evidently Zakicowi had made the threat often that he was going to use her as the stake in another game. "She seemed very relieved when I informed her that you don't gamble."

"Only with my life." Wyatt replied quietly.

"We have an object on the scanner." Taga called out, gaining everyone's attention. "Size and configuration resemble a shipping container."

"Space junk?" Pruit theorized, mostly to himself, but Wyatt still heard him.

"I wouldn't be the first time that one of these scumbags wound up with their hold too full to hold another container, and then strapped it to the outside of the ship with magnetic limpets." Wyatt grumbled, rubbing his chin. "Several have been known to come free when using those old attachment methods."

Still there was something bothering him about this particular container. He watched it on the screen for several seconds. It just sat there, a large steel box, hanging there in space. It didn't look threatening, it just sat there. It then hit him. *It's just sitting there.*

"What's the drift rate on that thing?" Wyatt pressed his copilot.

"Zero." Taga replied, a little confused.

"Full stop!" The captain ordered, to which Taga obeyed immediately.

"What is it?" Sonnet almost whispered to him.

"It's just sitting there." Wyatt waved his hand at the image on the screen. "No drift, no tumble, no rotation of any kind. That kind of thing doesn't happen by accident."

"It was placed there." Fox Pruit mused as the answer clicked in his mind. "It's a mine."

"Probably." Wyatt agreed. "At least that is what I'm thinking. Run an active ping scan. I want to know if there are more of these out there."

"An active scan may give our position away." Taga pointed out. Not to argue with his captain, but to point out the possible consequences of his actions.

"Can't be helped." Wyatt nodded at his alien copilot. "If we run into one of these, and it is a mine, it is going to ruin the rest of our trip."

Taga nodded and did a quick reconfigure on the scanners. He then started the active scan and his screen lit up.

"There are dozens of them!" Green stared in disbelief as she realized just how close they had come to getting blown out of space.

"Find the pattern." Wyatt barked to no one in particular.

"Judging distance, and calculating vectors, I would say that mathematically they are placed in a spherical pattern, with a hole in the center." Green replied, responding to Wyatt's command as if it were directed at her personally. "Distance ratios indicate 3.14159."

"Let me guess." Wyatt sighed. "The hole in the center is just barely large enough for the *Revenge* to fit through."

Taga's hands flew over his panel as he made some measurements and calculations.

"There is not much room for error." He finally announced, his math complete.

"Well Taga," Wyatt smiled at his partner. "This is your area of expertise. Your precision flying is probably better than mine. Take us in." Wyatt then looked around at his crew/business partners. "But first, let's get environmental suits on. Just in case."

"A prudent precaution." Taga agreed, as they all paused to retrieve and don suits, designed for working in space.

It only took a quarter hour for everyone to get properly suited up and regroup on the oversized bridge. Wyatt thought it a little strange, that Zakicowi had not removed bridge station positions, despite the fact that he had updated the controls to the point that most of those stations were redundant. But he was very glad that the alien pirate had left all the chairs and restraints in place. Now everyone was buckled in, and no longer just standing around. There were even a couple of chairs left over. It also gave his passengers something to do, as Kirby had made sure that all of the stations were fully functional. If Wyatt wanted he could assign people to the science station, communication station, helm, navigation and weapons, or he could simply run them all from the pilot or copilot position.

"What do you think are in those containers?" Pruit wondered aloud as the *Revenge* started getting closer to them.

"What would you put in them?" Wyatt asked his previously fellow Marshal.

"Kiln Nukes?" Fox replied as he rubbed his chin in thought. "Possibly Hyper-shock bombs. I wouldn't go for contact nukes, although they would be cheaper, the probability of them actually contacting the hull of a ship is slim. No, I'd go with something with a proxy detonation range."

Kiln nukes made sense to Wyatt, although they were prohibitively expensive. Hyper-shock weapons would make more sense. A hyper-shock going off at this range would turn every living thing aboard a ship to jelly, but leave the ship relatively undamaged. However, they too were very pricey. Contact nukes would wipe out a ship ten times the size of the *Revenge* like a bullet hitting a fly. They were also cheap and easy to come by. But they had to contact the skin of a vessel to really make their punch felt. With no atmosphere to carry the shockwave, they were less effective.

"Alright Taga." Wyatt sighed. "The ship is yours. Take us in."

"I have the con." Taga replied, in a formal sounding manner. "Ahead one quarter on thrusters only."

Wyatt fought the temptation to question that decision, even though in the back of his mind he knew it to be the correct one. His impulse engines worked on a gravity generation method and would probably start those makeshift mines moving in one direction or another.

The ship started to crawl forward. It was clear that with the speeds and distances involved it was going to take several hours to clear this field. To pass the time, he started calling up the scans of the moon to have something to study and take his mind off how nerve-racking piloting through a minefield could be.

CHAPTER 19

Wyatt hadn't realized that he had drifted off, but he awoke with a start. Fortunately for him, no one else seemed to have noticed. Everyone was riveted to the screen, watching the containers inch by. Instead of worrying about it, he just made a note of the time, and chalked himself up to being the ultimate calm and cool commander as everyone else was on pins and needles and he was sleeping. It was always possible that he was just lazy, but he was going to go with the cool and calm explanation. It was better for the ego.

"Scan update." Wyatt called out as he watched the last of the containers pass by.

"Scans show we are through the field." Green called out, as she had taken up a position at the navigation table. "We are approaching the moon at optimal docking speed and descending into a rather large crag in the surface."

"Stay on this course." Wyatt ordered, to which Taga nodded. "I have a feeling that we are going to find our back door directly in front of us. Keep scanning for artificial structures. Also look for holes in the scanner reply. Those will sometimes indicate pockets of atmosphere below the surface. He can camouflage his doorway, but he can't hide the hole behind it."

"Aye captain." Green called out. She then looked again at her screen and squinted. "I think I have a match. Scans show a blank spot on the return which I'm interpreting to be a pressurized space." She didn't know whether to be impressed or not at Wyatt's call. She then raised him a notch in her respect column.

The ship glided through the field of debris and crumbling fragments toward the area that was clearly artificial. The micro gravity of the moon making the handling of the ship, very easy and pleasant. Landing like this would be a simple matter.

"This isn't right." Green mumbled as she poured over her screen. "This can't be correct."

"What is it?" Wyatt raised an eyebrow as he heard the shock in her voice.

"There are modern structures here, that much is certain." Green began. "But they are built on top of something else. Something much older. Something that shouldn't exist."

Wyatt rose from his chair and transferred the image she was looking at to the main nav table. There a three-dimensional rendition of the scans she was looking at was constructed.

"No wonder this moon was always so unstable." Wyatt mused. "It's been hollowed out."

"Hollowed out?" Kenjay repeated. "By whom?"

"Probably by the same aliens that put Earth's moon in orbit so many millions of years ago." Green replied, in awe.

Mankind had been in for a shock when they finally got to the moon and started colonizing it in earnest. It turned out that the inspiration for so many poems, sonnets and love stories was, in fact, an abandoned alien research station that was covered in lunar dust. The realization that mankind wasn't alone in the universe turned out to one of the greatest catalysts to bringing people together. It also helped to jumpstart man's technology base and spurred our race to the stars. The question still remained though, of who were they? In all the years of space exploration, humans had not come into contact with any beings that were that much farther ahead of humans in technological development. No one knew what had happened to the aliens that were, at one time, spying on Earth. Had they moved on to a different region of space? Had they suffered some disease or other disaster and gone extinct? It was one of the great mysteries of space.

"Why has no one heard about this?" Green gasped, practically salivating at the thought of a new find.

"Well the first surveys out here were more concerned about the moons trajectory and if it posed a danger." Wyatt theorized. "They weren't too concerned about the moon itself, just where it was going. Then the pirates moved in, and it became a place too dangerous to explore. And the pirates probably weren't too concerned about archeology."

That comment earned a bit of a sour look from Green, not that she could dispute what he said. Still, if the Samurai Moon was now relatively cleared of the pirate menace, perhaps she could lead an expedition when this salvage job was over. Maybe Wyatt could even be talked into assisting. She didn't resist the thought of spending more time with the man. He wasn't unattractive, despite his lack of education or refinement. Not that she was all that refined herself. Still, she thought she cleaned up pretty good when she had to. At that thought, she spared a moment to imagine what Wyatt would look like in a neo-suit, and decided that she liked the image.

"I believe I have located the docking port." Taga announced, as he guided the ship in for a hard dock.

The docking point was such that it wouldn't allow for a complete landing, but the ship could be suspended with minimal use of the antigrav thrusters. This would, however, require the ship to remain powered. Which made it easier to detect, but also allowed for a quicker get away, should one be needed.

"Hard dock established." Taga's voice was almost mechanical now. He was doing what he did best, almost automatically. Still, he went by the checklist. He was just that kind of professional. "All pressures in the green. All lights are go and board reads good to go for a safe departure. There is atmosphere and pressure on the other side."

"Alright." Wyatt announced as he got up. "Kenjay, Sonnet, Fox and Annwyl are with me. Green, you and Taga keep the ship ready to go."

"But Captain." Green began to protest. "There are alien structures, artifacts and possible clues to their civilization down there. I can't stay here."

"You said that the new structures had been built on top of the old." Wyatt explained. "So the two probably don't mix anyway. For now, we stick to the plan and make this a fact-finding mission about the *Western Rose*. We are under the gun here and time is not on our side. I'm not insensitive about the prospect of exploring alien ruins, but that is second fiddle for now."

Green grumped, but said nothing Wyatt could hear. He then considered the matter closed they got down to business.

The team didn't believe that the environmental suits were necessary for the exploration of the pirate moon. That being the case, everyone wore what they were most comfortable with. Wyatt, however, did take the precaution of adding an impact resistant duster, much like Fox's. He figured a little extra protection couldn't hurt. Wyatt liked to think of himself as a healthy paranoid, which was a way of saying his precautions kept him alive.

Air hissed from the airlock as there was almost always a slight pressure differential between a ship and a station. But there was no resistance when the airlock hatch creaked open. Automatic lights came on, revealing a corridor cut out of the very rock of the moon. It was a light grey, highly polished and reflected the light brilliantly. Whatever else could be said about the ruthless, murdering, raping pirate, Zakicowi was obviously a neat freak.

Wyatt was convinced that Zakicowi's base would be boobytrapped somehow. The problem was he could see no way to deactivate anything that might be armed. There were no palm readers, key slots, key pads or RFID readers that he could detect anywhere. Not only that, but Annwyl strode through completely unconcerned. She, evidently, had never seen him deactivate anything that might do them harm.

"Annwyl?" Wyatt asked, quietly.

"Yes…captain." She replied with a little hesitation, still not used to the form of address she was supposed to use.

"Are you wearing any jewelry that Zakicowi gave you?" He pressed on. "Any item that he told you not to take off?"

"Well, other than my collar," She began, instinctively reaching up and touching her neck. "This bracelet is the only thing I've kept on." She held up her hand, and immediately Wyatt grabbed it and gave it a deep look.

Her bracelet looked like it was made of a dark, but beautiful wood. It caught the light and reflected a complex but lovely pattern. It was obviously delicately crafted and expensive.

"It's a tag." Wyatt whispered to the others as he showed them the reading he was getting on his hand scanner as he scanned the jewelry. "This is what is shutting off the traps." He tapped the bracelet for emphasis. "Stay close to her. No matter what. I don't care if we have to carry her. We get separated, it might be very bad, health wise, for us."

Nods were returned from both Fox and Sonnet. Even Annwyl seemed to understand that she needed to stay close to everyone.

"Annwyl." Sonnet whispered. "Is there some kind of command deck or operations center?"

"There is." She confirmed. "This way."

The group then started to follow, very closely, the former slave girl, hoping that she knew where she was going.

CHAPTER 20

They arrived at the command center, just in time to experience the first rattle of an impact, rocking the moon. As quickly as he could, Wyatt threw on scanners, looked over readouts and went over the weapons console.

"Curzo is hitting the place with long range impact lasers. Looks like he intends to bore his way through the main entrance." Wyatt informed the group. "We don't have much time. Fire up the records computers and download everything you can! I'm activating the active defenses. Let's see how they like it when they have to deal with more than just the passive systems."

Rockets or varying types, and lasers of different magnitude suddenly split space apart. Curzo had been making his way forward, using mobile construction pods to pick their way through another minefield and take out any defensive platforms. Now active defenses homed in on the much to close pods and wiped them away like chalk from a chalkboard. Sympathetic explosions, rocked outward from the shipping container mines that the pods had cautiously moved, or avoided. In an instant, dozens died, and Wyatt hadn't even gotten warmed up yet.

"We can't stay!" Annwyl shouted, suddenly.

Wyatt turned to look at the little girl, and saw the terror in her eyes. He knew, right then, something horrible was about to happen.

"What is it Annwyl?" Sonnet pried as she too registered the fear she was displaying.

Annwyl then pointed at a small blinking light on one of the panels.

"Master said that if I ever saw that I should run." She explained. "Grab Oso and run for the nearest escape pod."

"Good enough for me." Wyatt shouted in reply and immediately started toward the exit. He assumed it was some kind of self-destruct, and knew he didn't have the time to figure out how to disarm it. The only strategy that made sense from this point was retreating. The only question that kept playing in his mind was, had something they had done set it off, or was it the attacks from Curzo?

"We don't have all the data yet." Fox protested.

"If you want to stay for it, I'm not going to stop you." Wyatt replied, dripping with sarcasm. "But the rest of us are making for the *Revenge*."

Fox seemed to debate with himself, but not for very long. It was evident that Zakicowi had put some kind of dead-man switch in place to keep his secrets. Even from the grave the alien was incredibly annoying. Fox grabbed the data crystal he had been downloading to and shoved it into his pocket.

The group ran and stumbled as whatever self-destruct failsafe Zakicowi had installed began to make itself more prominently known. Explosions rocked the compound, doors that were meant to isolate different sections, slid open to allow atmosphere to escape or fire and destruction to spread.

"I really hope these explosions don't damage the alien architecture beneath us." Sonnet mumbled in a disconnected thought as they made their way toward their awaiting ship.

Wyatt shot her an odd look as her statement registered. But somewhere inside he understood the significance of the find, and secretly he too, hoped that they would remain intact.

It seemed to take forever, like it always does when running from danger, but finally, they reached the long straight hallway that lead to the docking connection. It was then that the atmosphere behind them failed. It wasn't the howling wind of a vacuum sucking at them, like it would have been had they completely lost pressurization somewhere. It was more like a slow leak. Akin to taking an unpressurized aircraft higher and higher until the occupants asphyxiate.

Like all qualified pilots, Wyatt had been required to experience this very thing. He had been put in a chamber and had the oxygen pumped out so he could learn to recognize the symptoms of low pressure/high altitude asphyxiation first hand. Just like in the trainer, his color vision had washed away, his head was light and a dizzy, and the edges of what he could see were beginning to turn black.

"Revenge!" Wyatt called out over his wrist com. "Open the hatch and set...O2...generators to max...i...mum."

"Roger." came the faint reply. But Wyatt couldn't tell who was speaking. He was that far gone already.

They could see the hatch open, and the first wave of fresh air, hit them like a euphoric breeze. It wasn't enough to sustain them, it was more like trying to breathe through a straw that was too small, but it was better than what they had been getting, and served to energize them slightly. Even if the effect was more psychosomatic than real. Seeing the end of the journey probably did more to revitalize them than the actual fresh air did.

Wyatt made sure he was the last in line as the group stumbled through the hatchway. He almost had to carry Annwyl through, as she partially collapsed, just short of the doorway. As he pulled her through, he too succumb to the exertion and lack of oxygen. The last then he saw before the blackness took him was a pair of boots, that shouldn't have been there.

CHAPTER 21

Wyatt woke in much the same predicament he had found his female companions in just a few days before. Except for the fact that his hands were tied up so high that his feet did not touch the floor. He didn't know how long he had been that way, but his arms and shoulders ached from the strain. His eyes were still heavy, but he forced them open, only to see one of Curzo's henchmen running off. Presumably to tell his captain that his prisoner was awake.

It didn't take long after that, for the gloating pirate to make an appearance.

"Bounty-Marshal Wyatt Toranado." Curzo called out as he sauntered into the hold.

Wyatt raised his head and grinned at the calling of his name. He then took the opportunity to look around. It was obvious that they were still on the *Revenge*, bound up in the hold. Most of the others were in the same state he was. Suspiciously missing were Sonnet and Fox.

"It would seem that you underestimated me." Curzo pointed out as he stepped close to Wyatt.

Wyatt considered kneeing or kicking the gloating captain, but thought better of it. A moment of satisfaction was probably not worth the beating or execution he would receive as a result. Probably.

It was then that Wyatt located the missing members of his crew. Sonnet and Fox where standing next to Curzo. The double cross had revealed itself.

"I see you prefer the company of pirates to that of honest workers." Wyatt growled as he ignored Curzo's bluster to speak directly to Sonnet.

"No Marshall, I prefer the company of my own kind to yours." Sonnet then dropped the frilly, western style dress she had been wearing to reveal black leather pants, a gun belt with cutlass strapped to it, a white French cuffed shirt and black leather vest. If she looked good before, she looked absolutely killer now. Which was appropriate, given the amount of people she had killed.

"Did your father know?" Wyatt asked in earnest. "Did he know that the ships he was searching for had been taken as pirate prizes by his own daughter? Is that what drove him?"

"He suspected." Sonnet, admitted. "All of those research trips of mine, just happened to line up with attacks on missing ships. He found the *Princess of Mars*, on his own, but that was what gave me my start. Discovering that the cruise liner had not fallen victim to an accident and was instead, pilfered by buccaneers, was one of the best kept secrets in the galaxy. Had the company let out that it wasn't an accident, the insurance wouldn't have paid. They would have been on the hook for every lawsuit, salvage expense, and payout themselves. So they paid my father handsomely to keep it quiet.

"As for me, I saw the power, the destruction, the sheer audacity of the pirates that had taken her. I knew then, that high space was for me. Still, my father had other ideas, and tried to educate the thoughts and fantasies out of me. It turned out to be the perfect cover. I would research, companies, people, cargos, and trade routes and feed Curzo and Zakicowi the locations and times to strike for the fattest prizes."

"And your father, would chase after these wrecks trying to find the truth." Wyatt observed. "Trying to learn, once and for all, if his daughter was working with pirates. He didn't go missing searching for the *Rose*, you killed him for his research. You killed your own father just for a map to buried treasure."

"*I* didn't kill him." Sonnet gave Wyatt an innocent look. "But he did meet his end searching for the *Rose*. He just had the displeasure of finding out that one of his people was more loyal to me than he was to him." Sonnet patted Fox on his shoulder to which he shrugged.

"You killed him." Wyatt gave Fox a look. "Too bad you didn't get the exact location out of him before he began to suspect you. That's why you needed me."

Both he and Sonnet shrugged in reply.

"Zakicowi's wrist com is actually what we required. That is, the minicomputer disguised as the beautiful wooden bracelet he wore, which was married to the computer on his base. Much like yours is to the AI onboard this vessel. I was afraid you would figure that out when Annwyl showed you hers. Fortunately, it didn't seem to click." Sonnet revealed. "*Your* AI put up quite a fight by the way. Too bad I had already taken steps to disable him while he was being repaired. That's probably why he seemed a bit twitchy as of late. When Fox downloaded the computer at the base, he wasn't simply taking everything like we wanted you to believe. He knew exactly what information and files he needed. We now have the location of the *Rose* and no longer need you."

"So what happened?" Kenjay called out from his position. "Did Zakicowi get greedy? Did he not share the location of where he had hidden the *Western Rose*?"

"That fool wanted to show he was better than a highly educated, part time pirate." Sonnet spat as she walked over to the hanging Samurai. "Better than a human female.

"He organized the raid on the Wells Argo stage himself. Claiming that the orders were coming from me. I had warned him off that particular cargo, because I knew the security would be too great. He, on the other hand, saw it as an opportunity to not only get out from under my command, but to wipe out most of the old clans in the process.

"His creativity actually impressed me." She admitted, although it pained her to do so.

"You only needed me to get Zakicowi's possessions to find out where he hid the ship. You just needed his wrist com. One little piece of information I probably would have sold or even given you, had you asked." Wyatt shook his head. "Now you, and your old business partner, reckon on finding it on your own and cutting the rest of us out."

"I plan on finding the *Rose* and taking back what is rightfully mine." Sonnet grumbled in return. "Zakicowi worked for me. I was, am, the pirate king. I made them all wealthy and he repaid me by keeping the fattest calf for himself."

"Then what happens to us?" Wyatt inquired, not liking the likely answers to that particular question.

"I must admit I struggled with the decision of what to do with you. You, Marshal, are far too dangerous to be kept around." Sonnet replied as she paced around him. "On the other hand, you might have information in your back pocket, which might prove to be useful. Still, I believe that the risk, outweighs the benefits. You're simply going to have to die."

"No!" Green shouted from her position near the rear.

"Oh don't worry dear." Sonnet informed her. "You'll be joining him. As will Taga. I can't afford to have qualified pilots around that might have ambitions about taking the ship. Ironically Mister Taga's presence here was an accident. He was the one that was supposed to be poisoned, not Asawa. Unfortunately, good help is hard to find and my man, poisoned the wrong samurai. Don't worry Master Kenjay, he will recover in time. The poison will only make him sick, not kill him.

"Speaking of Master Kenjay, well, he gets to stay. I need his business contacts to move the dark matter."

"What about Annwyl and Oso!" Wyatt demanded. Seeing that even the child was strung up with the rest of them.

"I'm not a monster." Sonnet cooed at Wyatt. "I've no designs on them. I can drop them back in Tortuga when we are finished. No one is going to take the word of an uneducated former slave and a samurai without a clan, over mine."

It was then that she nodded over toward some of the pirate crew and they began to move toward Wyatt, Green and Taga.

Sonnet turned back toward Curzo as the two walked over toward the airlock.

"We are short on crew." Curzo whispered to her. "We took too many loses attempting to gain access to Zakicowi's base."

"You were supposed to wait for my signal. You wouldn't have had to do anything had you just been obeyed your instructions." Sonnet growled back at him. "now we are down to one construction pod and only enough crew to man the *Revenge* and possibly move the cargo. We'll never be able to move the Rose with this small a crew."

"Also, my ship is older." Curzo protested. "It is manpower intensive, especially in combat or salvage operations. Zakicowi spent most of his credits updating and modernizing this ship. It is better equipped to handle what we are going to encounter. I believe we should limit ourselves to only bringing this vessel."

"And I suppose you are going to be wanting this ship when this is all over?" Sonnet raised an eyebrow at him, knowing that most of his reasons for taking the *Revenge* on this mission was to get a foothold on it. He wanted this ship.

"The thought had crossed my mind." Curzo admitted.

"Very well." Sonnet sighed. "You can even take the captain's cabin now. I still have my room onboard."

Curzo nodded and bowed slightly as she seemed to acknowledge him as captain and future owner of the *Queen's Revenge*. Although he knew he was deluding himself if he believed for on moment that she wasn't in charge at the moment. He might be captain, but she was the admiral of the fleet.

The pirate leader's attention was drawn back to Taga, Green and Wyatt as they were being marched toward the airlock. It was then that Taga struck.

Taga may not have been the greatest warrior, or the most proficient with a weapon, but that didn't mean he wasn't going to go down swinging. He stomped the foot of a guard that had gotten too close, then head butted him backward. Then, being bound in front like the others, grabbed the man's gun and started charging toward Wyatt. He plowed over two more guards on the way, and absorbed hits from multiple directions as he ran. Pain burst through his sides and shoulder as he was hit, but he didn't slow up.

Wyatt took advantage of the distraction to kick his guard square in the back. There was a satisfying snap as the man sailed forward into the bulkhead. Green likewise, kicked backward, striking her guard in the hands and knocking his blaster from his grip.

Taga could feel that he was almost spent. The pain and loss of blood overcoming his adrenaline rush. He used his last remaining strength to throw the blaster he had taken from the guard, to Wyatt. He then crumpled to the deck. Unmoving. He had died a hero worthy of song. A samurai's most noble goal.

Wyatt caught the weapon on the fly and dove behind some shipping crates. Green tumbled in right next to him, a blaster recovered from the guard she kicked, in her own hands.

"Let me get those." She shouted as she undid his bindings.

"Thanks." He replied as he quickly returned the favor, between shots.

"Options?" Green asked a she picked off a pirate trying to flank them.

"No good ones." Wyatt grumbled, two blaster bolts smashing into the crate, inches from him.

"Then let's go with bad ones." Green chuckled as she took another shot.

Wyatt motioned for her to follow him as he dashed toward the construction module hanging in its launch rack. Bolts flew past them wildly, but they were quick and there was a lot of cover in the crowded hold. Wyatt leapt up into the hatch and pulled Green up behind him. Once inside, she was quick to hit the button to seal the door, closing them inside.

"Now what?" Green grumped. "We're sitting ducks in here."

"Not exactly." Wyatt countered. "These construction modules are tough. They can shoot blasters at her all day, and won't make a dent."

"What about missiles?" Green pointed at a couple of men attempting to set up a portable launcher.

"Now those will make a dent." Wyatt shrugged.

He then pushed the controls forward and sent the module racing toward the hanger doors. Faces turned white as everyone realized he was about to smash through and expose them all to the vacuum of space.

Sonnet was the one that pressed the door release, and opened up the cargo hold door. Wyatt, then seeing his strategy was working. Flew through the airlock to take the proper way out of the ship, rather than punching a hole through the loading door. It took only seconds for the airlock to cycle, and soon Green and Wyatt were drifting clear of the ship and free to maneuver in the blackness of space.

"Great." Green grumped. "Now we are stuck outside of the ship in a short-range pod. What is your next move Napoleon?"

Wyatt didn't answer at first. He was too busy flying away from the ship as fast as he could.

"Oh don't worry," He replied. "It gets worse." He then pointed at the ship to ship guns mounted along the side of the ship. To which she nodded and spurred him onward.

He wagered it would take a couple minutes for the ship to clear for ship to ship engagement, and he didn't want to be in range when they did.

"First we need to know where we are." Wyatt indicated the nav computer, and Green obediently got on it.

"We're still near Samurai Moon." Green called out.

"Then let's head for it." Wyatt sighed. "Maybe there is something useful that survived."

Green fumed a bit, but said nothing. She didn't have a better idea and they had to do something. She only hoped it would be enough.

CHAPTER 22

The construction module was cramped as it was not designed for more than one person. Still the life support was adequate for the job and they weren't exactly stepping on each other.

Wyatt piloted the craft toward the same place that they had docked at before. Even though he knew that there would be no atmosphere there, he still needed to explore every option. Making it as far as Tortuga would not be one of them. Even making it to the moon was a stretch. The modules were designed to be used in conjunction with a mother ship. They were also purposely designed to not carry life support for more than twelve hours. This kept contractors from working too long or driving people past safe deadlines. With two people onboard, the life support was taxed even further, and although it could keep up with the demands of two people, it's operational life was cut in half.

Fortunately, Wyatt believed in being prepared for every eventuality. His equipment was in top notch condition. Pulling over to fix a repair in space, simply wasn't an option. Also, the module was equipped with redundancies, such as an extra environmental suit. There were even four extra tanks, when the normal requirement would have been two.

"We'll need to suit up." Wyatt reminded Green. "I'm also willing to bet our little escapade earlier has set those container mines into motion. I'm just hoping that their drift rate takes them away from the moon, and not towards it."

"That is the probable outcome." Green assured him. "We vented a lot of atmosphere and debris from the base. It more than likely knocked the mines away."

"Remind me to send a memo to the local Aids to Navigation Team." Wyatt quipped with a bit of humor. "They'll have to come out here and destroy those things as a hazard."

Truth be told, Wyatt was less than joking when he made that comment. He would feel awful if one of those mines drifted into an innocent vessel that just happened to be transiting the system. It was one of those Murphy's law things that as big and vast as space was, loose objects tended to find each other. It was also a law of statistical anomalies, that random events tended to cluster together. Usually in spectacular fashion.

"All sensor readings indicate that the way ahead is clear." Green informed him as she read the readouts. "You should have a straight shot at the docking point.

"Just what are you hoping to find, anyway?" Green was nervous and it was showing. She, of all people knew what they were searching for. A way to survive.

"What I'm really hoping to find is a fully fueled and supplied back up vessel." Wyatt wouldn't admit it, but right now he was grateful for the distraction of conversation as he guided the little module toward the docking point. "What I settle for is an escape pod. If you recall, Annwyl said her orders were to get to an escape pod. Hopefully there are still some there."

Green nodded, then fell silent. The thoughts of the alien relics were popping up in her mind. She knew it would be a fool's errand to even try to get a look at them now, but still it bounced into her thinking.

The pod docked with a thump and hiss as the airlock tried to pressurize. When it failed, red lights blinked and warnings appeared on readouts.

"No atmosphere." Wyatt mumbled.

"Were you expecting any?" Green shot him a sideways glance.

"Not really." He confessed to her. "But it would have been nice if some kind of automated maintenance protocol would have fixed them."

Green cursed at herself for not considering that possibility. Ships, stations, and bases like this were often replete with automated cleaners and maintenance robots that would fix most of the systems available. Most of them were routine in nature, but there were some bots available that could perform emergency repairs. With Zakicowi's apparent love of cleaning robots, it would seem to be a safe bet that there were some automated maintenance ones around as well. It was a pity that they either weren't functioning, or hadn't completed repairs yet.

Soon, both of the intrepid explorers had checked each other, grabbed the extra tanks, and started to make their way out of the pod.

"Where too?" Green's voice asked from over the suit to suit com link.

"Command center." His reply seemed obvious. "See if we can get a status on what, if any, systems are still working. Maybe we can call for help."

The two stepped out into the hallway and did have to dodge an automated repair bot as it went about its duty and attempted to repair the damage. Alas one of the things it had not gotten to yet were the lights, and Wyatt sighed as the automated lights failed to come on. Fortunately, the suits had their own headlights so it was not a show stopper. What turned out to be the big stumbling block was the hallway itself. They made it halfway to the command center before the floor gave way. Even in the reduced gravity of the moon the large section that fell away made it impossible for the two explorers to leap to safety. They both screamed as they cascaded downward, into darkness.

****

Kenjay awoke with a start. He did not even realize that he had been knocked out during the fire fight. One of Curzo's henchmen didn't want to take the chance on him becoming a threat as well, so he struck him while he was still helpless. Kenjay never saw the blow coming, not that he could have done anything about it if he did.

"Easy Master Kenjay." Oso comforted his new teacher.

Kenjay was forced to smile at the concern his student showed for him. Normally he fought his lessons, his restrictions and even Kenjay's very existence, tooth and nail. Now, with his fate intertwined with his teacher, he was being very polite indeed.

"What has transpired?" Kenjay asked as he sat up. His head throbbed, but it was nothing that wouldn't pass in a short time. Still, that did not make it comfortable now.

"That cowardly hairless dog has run off." Oso grumbled. "He chose to save his own skin rather than fight these braggarts."

"Would you have preferred that he died gloriously, under the guns of so many allied against him?" Kenjay gave him a look that should have melted the boy on the spot, but it simply bounced off his armor of loathing and anger.

"That would have at least had the semblance of honor." Oso stomped his foot as he rose and began pacing around the shipping container prison that they had designed for him.

"Honor would not help us." Kenjay pointed out. "Had he stood his ground he would have fought valiantly and died swiftly. Then how would our circumstances be changed? The captain, instead, is living up to the old axiom, He who fights and runs away, lives to fight another day."

"There will be no other day." Oso whined. "He will leave us to our fate."

"Annwyl?" Kenjay looked at the sullen young woman. "Do you believe the captain will come for us?"

"I believe he will make every attempt to do so." Annwyl declared in a quiet but firm voice. "If we do not see him again, it is because he is dead."

"Not a pleasant thought, but probably an accurate one. He told me once, that we are his crew." Kenjay smiled at the memory. "And a captain does not leave his crew behind, no matter how annoying they are." He gave a pointed look in Oso's direction at the last part. But he followed it up with a gentle smile. "In the meantime, since we cannot guarantee that our captain has survived thus far,

I believe that it would be prudent to work on saving ourselves."

"It would be much easier to do that if you had left me in my room." Oso grumbled.

Kenjay raised his brow as he considered the implications of what the boy was telling him.

"Are you saying you have means of escape in your quarters?" He finally asked the young one.

"I do." Oso admitted. "There are passages in the walls that are not in the ship schematics. Many nights I have held a blade to one of your throats, and many mornings I have cursed myself for not ending you."

"What stopped you?" Kenjay asked the boy.

"Where would I go?" Oso demanded, almost in tears. It was the first true emotion anyone had seen out of him. "What would I do? I have no clan, no skills, no occupation. I don't even have a father, thanks to that hairless dog!"

Tears burst forth as the boy, thanks mostly to his fear, finally faced the anger he had been using to fuel his bitterness and resentment. Normally Kenjay would have been delighted at this revelation, but at the moment it was a hindrance to their escape.

"That is exactly why you should count your blessings that someone like Wyatt Toranado found you." Kenjay nearly shouted, stunning the boy into silence. "I argued to throw you out into the street. The son of an honor-less pirate has no place dining at the same table with someone from the house of Kenjay. I am royal caste. Sword master of the ninth degree. My family has the honor of holding the keys of a thousand planets. I shouldn't even be on the same ship as you. But this man, the one you call a hairless dog, has not only taken in the son of an enemy, he has made it a condition of our partnership that I teach you in the ways of our people. He has saddled me with you, and I have agreed, because honor demands it. I should launch you out an airlock for even suggesting that Wyatt Toranado was anything less than saintly toward you.

"It's true." Both Oso and Kenjay turned toward the small female. "The captain was under no obligation to keep us onboard. But he did. He even arranged for me to have a percentage of whatever it is we are after. I also know that he came for me when he could have left Sonnet and myself behind. He is a better and more honorable man than I deserve to serve."

Both Oso and Kenjay were stunned. Not by her admission, but by the force behind it. Gone was the timid and shy slave that was afraid of offending anyone. Here stood a woman who would voice her opinions and not back down.

It took several moments for Kenjay to reassert himself and compose himself enough to continue. Even Oso took time to digest what Kenjay and Annwyl had said.

"So, now that it is all settled." He finally managed. "How do we go about extricating ourselves from this predicament?"

CHAPTER 23

Wyatt was relieved to look at his com and see that he had only been out for two minutes. Even Green was beginning to stir.

"What the hell just happened?" Green demanded as she got to her feet.

"I believe we have fallen into the ruins you wanted to explore." Wyatt revealed.

Green first felt a moment of exhilaration at the thought of being the first ever to explore these ruins, but it was quickly replaced with horror as she realized that they now were basically trapped in, what could be, an alien tomb. That is, if it wasn't a tomb before, it could very well turn into one now.

"As fascinated as I am by what I am seeing." She brushed herself off, as she rose to her feet. "I was really hoping that that we were going to find a fully fueled and ready ship in a hanger somewhere. If that was a bust, I was all for your idea of calling for help, or using the escape pods. Even if the thought of using one of those things scares me to death." She shuddered reflexively at the thought. "I used drop capsules several times in the corps and they always scared the hell out of me. And an escape pod isn't much bigger."

"Do you still have your extra tank?" Wyatt wanted to try to get her thought process back on task, and he was curious as his had bounced several feet away from him. Something that he believed should not have happened.

"No! Oh wait. Yes, I do." She walked over and picked up hers. "It's right here." Then then stopped and held it up a moment. "Why is it so heavy? For that matter, why am I so heavy?"

Wyatt reached down and picked up a piece of rock debris from the ceiling. He then threw it across the chamber, where is landed with a satisfying thump. A thump that shouldn't have existed.

"The gravity is different here." He then checked his wrist scanner and pulled off his helmet. "There's atmosphere too. This doesn't make any sense."

"The mass of this moon should not have been enough to trap a pressurized space like this." Green announced as she made some mental calculations. "Also, nothing like this showed up on the scans."

"Well we seem to be dealing with an alien technology." Wyatt returned as he looked around. "I'm not going to be putting any money on what's possible or not."

The enormous cavern they were in was beautiful to behold. Wherever the floor hadn't been damaged by falling debris, it was highly polished with a marble like appearance. There were columns of the same polished stone every fifty feet. What surprised them was that there were no carvings, no hieroglyphs or anything that would mark or label this spectacular place.

"This is all carved out of solid stone." Green gasped. "This wasn't built here, it was carved into the moon itself."

"Well you wanted to explore this place." Wyatt waved around him in emphasis. "You lead on."

"Well there has to be something here." Green shrugged. "We might as well find it."

The two explorers picked a direction where the cavern narrowed and started that way. It was going to be a long walk, by the looks of things.

****

"Oso, what kind of weapons do you have in your room?" Kenjay asked of the devious youth.

"Knives mostly." He replied, a little disappointed in himself for not having a better stocked armory. "But I do have at least one ceremonial sword there as well."

Kenjay's eyes brightened at that. Most ceremonial swords were just that, ceremonial. They looked extravagant, but were mostly pieces of junk as far as combat went. But some, were as functional as they were beautiful. He only hoped that it was one of those, but even a junk sword was better than no sword.

"Annwyl." Kenjay whispered to the nervous young woman. "How many men do you think he has with him?"

"By my count he has twelve, not including Curzo, Miss Sonnet or Mister Pruit." She replied, indicating that she had been mindful to try and keep count.

"So what is the plan?" Oso inquired, nervously curious.

"First we remove ourselves from the confines of this prison." Kenjay replied, as if stating the obvious. "Then we allow ourselves to be captured."

CHAPTER 24

After, what seemed like, hours of walking the two started finding areas that looked less sterile and clinical and more functional and mechanical. They had passed grand halls, throne rooms, conference rooms, and a myriad of other empty rooms that looked like they could be small meeting rooms or large quarters, but now they were approaching the guts of the operation.

"What do you make of this?" Green asked as they entered a room full of cabinetry and flat surfaces.

"Kind of reminds me of a kitchen." Wyatt replied as he checked cupboards. "No food though. Not even the dust of any food."

"This place just reminds me of the treaty rooms of SanQuien." Green offered as she too began to check the pantry and cabinets.

"You mean the city that was built to hold the peace conference that was never used?" Wyatt searched his memory, hoping he found the right bit of information.

"Yes, that's the one." Green confirmed. "They built the entire city so that there would be neutral ground for both the Montana Freemen and the Planetary Alliance Body to hold their peace negotiations. Unfortunately, the Montana Freemen launched their planetary strike before it could be put to use. Both sides ended up destroying each other. The city is still sitting there, empty. Being constantly kept up on by an army of robots all set on automatic, but no one lives there. Too far outside of normal shipping lanes and it has no resources of any value. It can't even sustain farming."

"I remember now." He chuckled. "An entire state of the art facility, put where it was because no one would fight over it, now sits empty. Too expensive to let it rot away, too unsustainable to colonize. Government waste at its finest."

"I agree." She joined his laughter. "But this place strikes me as much the same way. Almost as if they were building it for something and never moved in. It's just odd."

"Could it have been built by an automated system?" Wyatt wondered aloud. Not really thinking she would have an answer.

"Possibly." She shrugged. "But whoever, or whatever was building this place, they probably wanted a way to communicate off of it. There are probably also heating and oxygen plants still running down here. There has to be some kind of command and control facility somewhere."

"It looks like we are heading the right way then." He confirmed as he pointed down the hall toward more mechanical looking rooms. "I figure they wanted to keep all the workings out of sight of the big ceremonial places. So, the farther we get from them, the more likely we are to find our control center. Maybe even a spaceport with a ship or two."

"Well that's optimism for you." She laughed.

"If you're going to be dreaming anyway," He winked at her. "Dream big."

****

"What does the lock look like to you?" Kenjay asked his student.

"Biomechanical." He answered as he looked over what he could see of the lock. "Palm scanner most likely."

"So it requires power to function." The master observed.

"Agreed." Oso couldn't quite grasp where his master was heading, but he was at least trying to work out his thinking.

"So if it requires power at a set rate, what do you think will happen if we change that rate?" Kenjay gave Oso a look that indicated that he wanted him to work it out for himself.

"The lock may either overload and blow open, become disconnected because of lack of power, or could seize all together." The young boy answered correctly.

"We shall hope for either the disconnection or the blowing of the lock." Kenjay chuckled. "It would be less than optimal to have the lock seize on us."

"What are we going to use for power to overload the lock?" Oso inquired as he looked around.

"The shock collar around your neck should suffice for that." The master then stepped toward the boy who retreated a step.

"But without the proper tools to remove it, the collar will shock me." Oso complained.

"Only if I had turned it on." The older alien smiled at the boy.

Oso's jaw dropped at the realization he could have removed the collar at any time. His teacher had only activated it during those moments when he knew that he would attempt some kind of mischief. It said a lot about how well Kenjay had learned to read his character. Not something that was good for a twelve-year-old's ego.

It took almost an hour for Kenjay to take apart the collar and carefully remove the capacitor. It took another hour for the master to find a moment where he felt comfortable making the attempt. The guards were not plentiful, but the few they had were around often enough to keep a close eye on the prisoners.

"I wonder what Marshal Toranado would say at a moment like this?" Kenjay wondered aloud as he moved the leads of the capacitor into position.

"Probably, 'Here goes nothing.'" Annwyl observed from her position as lookout.

Kenjay actually paused to ponder the accuracy of her statement. He soon decided that she was entirely correct.

"Well then, in his honor, here goes nothing."

He touched the leads to lock and the arc across the gap burned a brilliant, but very small, white. There was even an audible crack as the electricity burned the air between the two points. The lock couldn't take the jump in power and little wisps of smoke began to escape its casing.

It took a few seconds, probably about five, but soon the lock hung free and could be moved out of the way.

"Easy as cobbler." Kenjay announced as he walked out of their makeshift jail. "Or was it cake?"

"It's pie." Annwyl corrected the sword master. "Easy as pie."

"No." Kenjay replied, a wistful look on his face. "I like cobbler better. Maybe even a good berry crisp."

"Do we really have time to debate this?" Oso demanded as he looked around.

"Quite right boy." Kenjay agreed. "The object is to get caught. But not just yet."

With that little detail out of the way, the group started making their way toward the boy's quarters. They just hoped that they wouldn't encounter too many ruffians along the way.

CHAPTER 25

Wyatt and Green finally started finding things that looked more and more mechanical. Stone floors gave way to metal, white walls turned to steel grey and light that seemed to come from everywhere, was now emitted by fixtures on the walls.

"This looks familiar." Wyatt muttered as they made their way forward.

"If you are going to say we've been going in circles, so help me." Green grumped, in an exhausted response.

"No." Wyatt replied, still looking around trying to put his finger on what he was seeing. "We've not been this way before, but the layout, the setup it's all so familiar."

Suddenly they turned a corner and came against a large door. It was metal, secured, and had writing in language they couldn't decipher across the top.

"What do you think it says?" Green asked as they looked up at it.

"If my gut instinct is correct." He replied, not taking his eyes off of it. "It says 'Bridge'."

Green's mouth fell open at the revelation. She hadn't considered for a moment that they had somewhere made a transition from some kind of station to a ship. But it did make perfect sense, in a way. If you were going to build a base out of a moon, you would first need transportation to get there. That ship you arrived in would have to serve as living quarters and the main support structure until enough of the moon was converted to serve as an operable base.

"So where is everyone?" She looked around at the immaculate bridge and began walking from station to station. "What happened?"

Wyatt didn't answer at first. He simply walked over to what looked like the captain's chair and sat down. *Millions of years and a completely alien species and yet ship design seems to follow the same principles.* Wyatt mused as he began looking over the buttons on the captain's console. He finally chose a combination that seemed correct and waited.

Lights on the bridge began to flicker, and screens started to come to life. Then the alien captain appeared on the large view screen in the center of the far wall. It was a beautiful creature to behold, smooth white skin, that almost glowed, large almond shaped, dark eyes, and head that came to a rounded point. It had no nose or ears that were visible and seemed to not be wearing any garments.

Green was in awe of what she saw, and heard.

At first the alien began speaking in, what they perceived to be, its native tongue, but then Wyatt called out an order.

"Earth Standard!" He voiced to no one, and yet the computer responded.

"Earth Standard, update 2550." The computer replied in a less than automated sounding voice.

"How did you know to do that?" Green demanded.

"I figured that if there was power to the system, that maybe it was receiving automatic updates from somewhere." He shrugged. "I thought it was worth a try anyway."

"Captain Tilak" The image on the screen began. "Ship's record. Our hollowing out of the moon has not gone according to plan. Scans did not reveal the presence of unstable fissures before construction. We have suffered multiple collapses and sustained casualties as a result. This has knocked the moon off of its orbit and it will now break away from its primary in only a few hundred years.

"I must admit, that I was taken aback by seeing the first one of our kind dead in some millennia. To know that I am ultimately responsible for the death of a friend, has shaken my confidence.

"I have since ordered a halt to construction. I have judged the resources that would be required to move the moon back into a stable orbit to outweigh any scientific value gained by using this observation post.

"Also, I must regretfully report that the collapses we have suffered have trapped our vessel. I fear that attempting to free ourselves would only result in the moon's complete destruction. Since that is the case, our plan is to abandon the *Pengould*, and return on the next resupply shuttle. If I am over ruled by the council and they wish to continue this endeavor we can return to our posts and resume our work. If the council agrees with my decision we then can return and retrieve the *Pengould* without concern for further damaging the moon.

"Until the next supply shuttle arrives, we shall remain in suspended animation and leave the ship on basic housekeeping duties. I only hope we experience no further unpleasantness. Losing my friend has made me long for home. Hopefully the thousand-year wait for the resupply shuttle will dull my pain." The image then faded from the screen, leaving a deafening silence on the bridge.

"I guess they decided not to continue their work on the moon." Green finally observed, breaking the hovering silence.

"Maybe." Wyatt punched in some commands, cursed, then punched them in again differently. At that point, a ship schematic appeared on the screen.

Wyatt then shot up and strode off the bridge and started making his way down to an area he had highlighted on the screen. The whole way down, Green was two steps behind, demanding to know where he was going and why. She was frustrated at apparently being ignored by him, but continued her questions.

All of her answers and Wyatt's fears were confirmed when they stopped just outside a doorway with more of the alien script over it.

"If you don't know what this one says," Wyatt whispered. "You will in a moment." Wyatt then hit the panel next to the door and it slid open.

Green stopped dead in her tracks as they entered the chamber. The room was huge, extending fifty feet high and three times that around. But what really stopped her dead was what was stacked inside that room. Cryogenic tube after tube, dozens of them were laid out in a circular pattern extending out from the middle. And each one of them contained the withered body of a dead alien.

****

Kenjay walked down the corridor, like absolutely nothing was the matter. He even bowed to those he passed, giving them a hardy greeting and continuing on. He chuckled at the thought of being a fly on the wall when the crew were reprimanded for letting him move about unchallenged. A few raised a questioning glance, or opened their mouth to say something, but then they must have come to the conclusion that if he had made it this far, he must belong here. It was not until he sauntered onto the bridge that he finally got a reaction.

Curzo turned, in his command chair, toward the sound of the opening door to the bridge. At first a look of mild annoyance at the disruption crossed his face, which was quickly replaced with a look of shock as he realized that Kenjay had no guards anywhere near him. In fact, he was flustered to point of babbling like an idiot.

"Master Kenjay if you have come here to beg…um…wait…are there no guards with you?" Curzo sputtered. "How the hell did you…why did you…Who let you out?"

"Oh no one let me out, captain." Kenjay revealed with a bow. "I just thought it would save time if I let myself out and came to you directly. You and I are both people who dislike it when little people get in the way."

Curzo couldn't argue with him there. He was not the type who liked to depend on underlings, this being just one more example of why not to.

"You don't fail to impress, Master Kenjay." Sonnet rose from her position off to the side of the bridge. "So, what brings you here."

"Speaking of underlings." Kenjay locked eyes with Curzo for the dig that made the pirate's blood boil. Fortunately for him, he held his tongue and said nothing.

"I have come to you seeking a deal, as it were." Kenjay bowed to the woman in charge.

"You have precious little to bargain with." Sonnet laughed.

"On the contrary." Kenjay disagreed. "I have the business contacts through which the dark matter can be distributed. Without me, you may be able to unload the cargo, but at a severely diminished price. With me, you might even be in a position to claim the *Rose* as legitimate salvage and not a pirate prize. After all, you yourself said that you weren't in on the original high-jacking. That Zakicowi acted on his own."

"If that's true, then why do I need your conduits?" She raised an eyebrow at him. "I'm sure the right people will come to me."

"Eventually, possibly." Kenjay concurred. "That, however, will take time. There will also be the possibility that your claim will be challenged. Possibly by Wells Argo, or maybe their insurers.

"But with someone with my business standings, contacts and means to distribute the booty and legally collect the payments, any challengers will find it difficult to make a claim. We might even have the entire cargo sold and distributed before they even know to file a challenge."

"So once again, I have the knowledge and resources to make this expedition worthwhile, while you have the contacts to make it highly profitable." She nodded at his basic premise. "So what is your proposal?"

"A third of the dark matter cargo." Kenjay stated flatly.

Curzo laughed, and even Sonnet shook her head.

"I was thinking more like ten percent." Sonnet replied, indicating that even that amount was being generous.

"I can hardly go back to my business partners and tell them we left to find the *Rose* as a team, a fact that they are well aware of, but I could only claim ten percent of the cargo for myself." Kenjay shrugged. "That would raise questions. The kind of questions we are trying to avoid."

Sonnet rubbed her chin at his analysis. What he was saying, certainly made a good deal of sense.

"You may also be overlooking one thing." He revealed, to which her head shot up.

"Enlighten me."

"The financials onboard the *Rose*. That stage was not only carrying the Baryonic dark matter, but also the credits for an entire banking operation." Kenjay prodded. "Their cover story of shifting a bank wasn't just a story. If you want proof of that, Wells Argo did continue with their plans and opened up that bank, six months later. The Rose doesn't just have the dark matter on board, but it has the credits of an entire banking operation onboard. I'll make no claim to that. You may keep it all. I just need the dark matter to not only retain our cover, but to appease my investors."

It wasn't as if Sonnet was in the dark about the credit shipment he was referring to, she had just become so focused on the dark matter that she had become blind to it. With his reminding, she now shifted her focus and broadened her horizon.

"Alright Master Kenjay." She agreed. "You'll have your third. Of the dark matter only. We keep the credits."

"There is one more request." He announced, to which he was given a suspicious eye.

"And that is?" Sonnet pressed.

"Our accommodations are less than stellar." He chuckled a bit. "We would like to be moved into Oso's room."

"Why his room?" Curzo asked with a suspicious eye.

"Because he is familiar with it. It is large enough, and judging by the size of your crew, you have probably assigned all of the other quarters." He smiled as he laid out his reasons point for point.

"I think something can be arranged." Sonnet replied, to which Kenjay humbly bowed.

CHAPTER 26

"He's playing us." Curzo griped as he watched the three new partners settle into Oso's old quarters.

"Perhaps." Sonnet agreed. "But he is correct in his analysis. With him as our witness, we'll be able to claim legitimate salvage rights on the *Rose*. He will also be able to increase our profit margin on the dark matter."

"Increase our margin?" Curzo spat in disbelief. "Increase it how? You're giving him a third of it."

"Yes, but we are increasing the size of the pie from which that third comes." Sonnet pointed out. Not that she thought he was getting what she was talking about. "Sixty percent of billions is more than ninety percent of millions."

Curzo grumped, but wisely did not press the matter. Just like he didn't press her decision to honor Wyatt's agreement to cut in Annwyl. Sonnet believed she had been through enough at the hands of Zakicowi and she had earned her share. There was also the fact that she basically saved her life back at Zakicowi's base. True, she had made certain things more uncomfortable for her. Curzo had to play up the kidnapping a little more than she had wanted him to, in order for Annwyl to not get suspicious. Also, that idiot henchmen had almost killed her, because he had no idea what was going on. Still in any enterprise like this one there were always risks.

Those risks were what drove Sonnet. The excitement, the passion. A pirate's life for her. It was a strange frontier when she stopped to consider it. A mix of high-tech western, alien Samurai and space pirates. All the makings for a bad novel if ever there was one. Maybe someday she would write it all down. It might even sell a few copies.

"I still say he's going to betray us." Curzo grumbled. "He's too honor bound not to."

"I have considered that." Sonnet agreed. "The problem is, for him, that his honor is divided at the moment. He has his commitments to his investors, his agreement to me, and his obligation to seek what is best for the boy. That part stems out of his agreement to Wyatt."

"And his other agreements to Wyatt?" Curzo gave her a look that asked a million questions without speaking.

"Wyatt escaped in an overloaded construction pod, designed for operation of no more than twenty-five-thousand-clicks from a support vehicle." Sonnet pointed out. "That pod has a maximum speed of *maybe* one-hundred-thousand-KPH. Do you think, even he, could have piloted that thing all the way to Tortuga?"

"That would be highly doubtful." Curzo admitted.

"I thought so." Sonnet agreed. "No, Bounty-Marshall Wyatt Toranado is somewhere dead in space right now. There was no place left for him to go, and no one to ride to his rescue. It's kind of a pity really. I could have used a man like that."

"You have a man like that." Curzo pointed out her partner, Fox Pruit.

"Fox is good." She admitted with a smile that indicated that Fox was good at a lot of things, some of which could be highly pleasurable. She always wondered if her father had known that she and Fox were lovers. Maybe that was why he always wanted him along, to keep him away from her. But that was something she would never know for sure. "But he's not as level headed or as smart as Wyatt was. It would be interesting to see the two go up against each other. But I wouldn't want to bet on the outcome."

"Hmmmm." Curzo suddenly indicate that his attention was elsewhere. "We have picked up our sensor echo again."

"I recall, Taga mentioning that." Sonnet walked over to look at Curzo's display. "Is it always there?"

"It comes and goes, but always at exactly the same spot." Curzo grumped. "I believe Taga to be correct that it is only a sensor ghost, it just sticks in that one spot too perfectly."

"Well, keep an eye on it." Sonnet sighed. "We don't need to be chasing ghosts, but I still want to know about it."

"I wholeheartedly agree with you there." Curzo then returned to his duties.

****

"Alright, here goes nothing." Wyatt warned as he gently pushed the power levels up on the alien ship. "Hold on, this might get a little tricky."

175

Learning the controls and operations of the alien vessel had been easier than he thought. The onboard computer was very intuitive and anticipated most of his demands. User interfaces were simple point and click, some of which were compatible with thought and interfaced neatly with Al. Even though the version of Al he had contained in his wrist com was incomplete the alien ship's computer seemed to fill in the gaps. Al worked just like he had on the *Revenge* or the *Stallion*.

The alien ship shuddered as it strained to pull away from the moon that had been its home for so long. Large chunks of rock bounced off the sturdy hull but still managed to make a cacophony of noise. Screeching sounds of the hull dragging across the surface was prevalent as millions of years of dust and debris were shaken off like water from a wet dog. It was nerve racking and seemed to take forever, but eventually the noise faded, the reflected light from the surface dimmed, and once again stars and the blackness of space shone before them. They were free, and clear to navigate.

The moon, was not so fortunate. It collapsed in on itself, just as the alien commander feared it might. It was a sad indication that any alien ruins left behind would now have probably been destroyed. It saddened both Green and Wyatt, but it was necessary for their survival.

"We are free of the moon and ready for course projection." Green announced from the station she had selected to use as a navigation terminal. "So where are we going?"

"We're going after the *Revenge*." Wyatt answered flatly.

"I was afraid you were going to say that." Green replied. "May I remind you that we are basically in a million-year-old alien terraforming and mining vessel, we're still not sure how a lot of these systems really work, and, oh yeah, we don't know where the *Revenge* is going."

"Al." Wyatt called out to his autopilot.

"Breadcrumbs, captain?" Came the reply from the A.I.

"Affirmative." Wyatt grinned as he replied.

"Breadcrumbs?" Green repeated, before the realization hit her. "You were leaving a trail. That's why you had to use the com center in Tortuga."

Wyatt just shot her a sideways smile, but said nothing to dispel her notion or confirm it. He just let her wonder.

****

Kenjay moved the secret panel, Oso had revealed to him, out of the way and looked inside. There he found a myriad of knives, and other melee weapons. Unfortunately, there were no blasters, or other projectile weapons. Evidently Oso's father had not gotten to that portion of his weapons training yet. Then he saw what he was after. The sword. It was beautiful and ornate. It also bore the mark of the House of Nishiro. One of the best sword makers in the known universe and the one that made Kenjay's own blade. This blade was not simply decorative, it was also deadly. It also bore another mark on the blade. The house of Tornonito. One of the clans related, by marriage to Kenjay's own. It was fitting that such a blade be used to extricate himself from this predicament. He would make sure to bring honor upon it.

"I only wish that I had access to your father's blade for you." Kenjay laid a hand on Oso's shoulder as he spoke.

"Oh not to worry." Oso consoled. "I stole that back from your quarters days ago. It's in the panel right next to your room."

The look of shock that appeared on Kenjay's face was palpable.

CHAPTER 27

"The navigation computer indicates that the *Rose* is probably hidden in the *Cook* asteroid field." Curzo informed his admiral.

A projection of the field appeared at the nav console. It was a very large asteroid field with ship destroying pieces of rock and iron spread over several astronomical units.

"Don't his files narrow down the search area?" Sonnet demanded. "We could be years searching all the large enough asteroids, that's even assuming we could through the field to get to them."

"All the file says as to the location of the ship, is that finding it will be easy as pie." Curzo replied with a grump of his own. "Not very specific instructions."

Sonnet looked at the course lay outs and studied them in silence for quite a while. The information they had, clearly guided them to the exact spot they were now sitting. It gave nothing further.

"We are in the right location." Sonnet thought out loud. "What more is there to this?"

"I don't know." Curzo admitted. "And we have no pods to send out to increase our search capability."

"Whose fault is that?" She glared at her captain, who wisely said nothing.

She finally got up and paced. She was trying to solve the riddle, but the answer wasn't jumping out at her.

"Start a grid pattern scan." She finally ordered him. "Maybe we'll get lucky. I know this field is going to make straight line searches impossible, but do the best you can.

"Has our sensor echo returned?"

"It was there when we made our approach to the field, right in the same spot as it was before." Curzo answered. "But as the dust and micro debris from the field increased, the shadow faded."

"Good. It was probably just a ghost then." She sighed in relief. "We don't need something else going wrong."

Curzo nodded, and started punching in the various commands. He then watched her leave as she stormed off the bridge.

****

Kenjay, Annwyl and Oso were officially confined to quarters, but that did little to slow down their wandering of the ship. Oso's revelation that there were secret passages had allowed them to come and go, pretty much as they pleased. They had even managed to acquire more knives, extra food, and some other miscellaneous items.

"I do wish we were able to get our hands on something with better range." Kenjay griped as he looked over their inventory of weapons. "But I'm afraid that one of these pirates would miss their blaster, more than they are likely to miss a couple of knives."

"I did retrieve my father's sword." Oso offered as he turned it over in his hands. "It might not be much, but it is something."

Kenjay patted the boys shoulder in a show of appreciation and support. He understood the boy's desire to use that sword in an attempt to avenge his father, possibly gain back his stripped honor and get a little revenge of his own. Unfortunately, he couldn't see a way to take on these pirates and be successful at taking the ship. There was also the added problem that if he managed to take the ship, who would pilot it. He was certainly no aviator and he had seen no such aptitude from the boy.

"I'm afraid I will not be of much use to you in the near future." Annwyl voiced quietly from her position, sitting on the bed.

"Nonsense my child." Kenjay replied, confidently. "When the time comes, you will play an essential role. But until that time, we must familiarize ourselves with these passages. We must be prepared to be able to move in complete stealth and darkness. Preparing for every eventuality is a must."

Both Oso and Annwyl nodded enthusiastically. They were willing to do whatever was required of them to take the ship back, or failing that, making the pirates pay for it in blood. A very heavy price indeed.

****

"Coming up on *Cook's* belt." Green announced as she read off the approach vector on her screen. "Running passive scans."

Wyatt grunted in acknowledgement. Secretly he doubted that keeping the scans on passive would allow them to remain hidden. They weren't a warship, they were a mining vessel. It was a massive ship and not exactly designed for stealth. They were also slow and difficult to maneuver, compared to the *Revenge*, and had very little in the way of offensive weaponry. The advantage they had was the toughness of their vessel. Since the ship had been designed for mining and construction, the hull was incredibly thick and made of a metal that Wyatt didn't recognize. It could probably stand everything that the pirates could throw at her and keep on coming. The other great advantage it had, was that if it could get close enough and grab onto the *Revenge*, they could rip it apart with massive claws and cut it up with powerful boring lasers.

"Where are they?" Wyatt whispered, more to himself than to Green.

"I've got them." Green called out, throwing her screen onto the main viewer. "They appear to be doing a grid search of the asteroid belt. It's going to take them a long time to find the *Rose* at that speed."

"Maybe." He mostly agreed. "But there's always the luck factor." Wyatt then studied the course the *Revenge* was taking. "Tactical options?"

"None." Green shot back with a disgusted look on her face. "This bucket is tough, but she's slow and handles like she's traveling through syrup, not space. We would have a chance if we could get close enough, but as it is the *Revenge* could run circles around us for hours and take potshots until they hit something critical."

"What if we made them come close to us?" The marshal was rubbing his chin in thought. His brain working a mile a minute.

"And why, exactly, would they come to us?" Her face was an interesting mix of emotions. She was desperately trying to work out his strategy while trying to point out there was no reason for the enemy to get that close to the ship.

"Well…what are they looking for?" Wyatt gave her the eye.

"A big ship." She answered. She knew she was missing something. The answer was there, hovering just outside of her grasp.

"And what are we in?" He waved his arms around as he asked.

"A bloody big ship." She replied, a wolf's smile making an appearance on her face.

"Set a course for half an AU in front of them." He put on a smile that matched hers. "Then put us on the biggest asteroid you can find in their path.

"While we wait for them, I'm going to record a message in the captain's log, set up some of Al's security protocols and start learning how to use the bells and whistles on this tub. We're going to need every trick to pull this off."

"Hey, your luck has held so far." Green encouraged. "We're still alive when we shouldn't be."

"Well then, let's keep it going." At that the two got to work. They had a plan to finalize, and ship to learn, a computer to program, and not much time to do it.

CHAPTER 28

It took less time than Wyatt would have thought to get the ship into position. Green masterfully maneuvered the large craft and set it down on one of the larger and more stable asteroids. There was a moment of concern when several alarms and scanner readouts all started to go off, but it turned out that they had left the mining scanners on, and it was giving them the readouts of the asteroid configuration.

"Well that was quicker than I thought." Wyatt complimented as he looked at Green. "That gives us more time to educate ourselves about this thing."

Green sighed in relief as she shutdown the unnecessary systems. "Do we have any water on this thing?"

"Actually yes." He replied, pulling up a schematic. "The water tanks were fully stocked and read as pure and potable. No food onboard though. All of that was automatically jettisoned when it began to spoil. We've also exhausted what was in the emergency stores of the construction pod. We are going to have to go hungry for the next week, when he head back toward Tortuga."

"That's ok." She laughed. "Give me a chance to lose those last stubborn five pounds."

He smiled as he tapped a couple keys that lit the way to one of the personal areas of the ship. In other words, the floor lit the way to the bathroom.

"Thanks." She then stretched as she got up and then quickly made her way off the bridge.

Wyatt waited for her to get clear of the bridge.

"Al." He called out to his A.I.

"Yes captain?" Al replied, sounding almost bored. Which was his usual sounding voice as he was almost always bored.

"Have you figured out the coms?" Wyatt had not had time to worry about talking to anyone, so he assigned that chore to Al. "And do we have enough power to send a hyper-cable?"

"Yes, on both counts." Al replied with a sense of triumph. Modesty was not one of this AI's virtues. "I have all coms functional on various frequencies and despite the years of inactivity the power levels are still at seventy-three percent."

"Wow." Wyatt was impressed. "Millions of years trapped in that rock, and still has a power reserve that high. This things reactor must be uber efficient."

"So it would appear." Al replied, as if stating the obvious. "This vessel is efficient enough that it can operate with power levels as low as twenty percent without activating protocols that would start shutting down non-critical systems."

Even that might be a generous amount of power. Wyatt was betting that even at twenty percent power this ship would still make it halfway across the galaxy.

"Al, I want to set up a series of broadcasts in the event something goes wrong." Wyatt explained. "I want them on local and long-range broadcast and I want them on this frequency." He plugged the frequency in manually so there would be no misunderstanding. "I also want it set up so, even if you are damaged or overwritten, the message will broadcast automatically."

"What would you like the message to say?"

Wyatt then began to type out exactly what he wanted Al to broadcast. It was part emergency beacon, part warning, and part explanation. And if it made it to the people Wyatt had designed it too, things could get sticky for anyone on board.

****

"Master Kenjay." Oso voiced as he stood before his teacher in the room that had become a porous prison. "I must confess a slight feeling of apprehension about our plan."

Kenjay smiled at the boy. It was the closest thing the he was going to get to saying he was afraid.

"I too approach our Rubicon with a bit of trepidation." Kenjay confessed.

"Rubicon?" Oso's face was that of confusion at the reference.

"It is an old human expression." The teacher began. "There was once a mighty general on Earth who wanted to take over an empire called Rome. As long as he stayed north of a river, called the Rubicon, he was not in violation of the law. But as soon as he crossed it, his decision to take his army to war was clear and undeniable. It marked a point of no return, as it were. There are reports that the general agonized over the decision. Finally, he made his decision. He crossed the Rubicon. Of course, he did it literally and we must only do it figuratively."

"So when do we cross?" Annwyl asked as she stretched.

"Now that is the question, isn't it?" Kenjay mused. "I do not know, child. What I do know is that we must be vigilant and poised to strike. I know not when we will get the chance to take that opportunity, but we must be ready for it."

"We will be." Both of the young ones replied in unison.

****

"I think we might have something." Fox called out from his position at one of the scanner stations. "I'm getting a reading."

Sonnet had almost forgotten that Pruit was a qualified pilot and had been trained by some of the same people that taught Wyatt to captain a ship. It was just that Pruit had never had the inclination, or capital, to obtain his own ship. He was fine with letting other people provide the carriage and undertake the expense of ship owning. Sure, it made for some awkward trips, especially when he was traveling with a bounty in restraints, but he made it work.

"What is it?" Curzo called out from the command chair.

"Not a definite lock yet." Fox explained as he squinted at the readouts. "Still too far out. But it looks like there is possibly a ship on the asteroid at quarter point port."

Sonnet and Curzo both got up and walked over toward Fox's station. He then called up the image as best he could.

"It's definitely a possible." Curzo mumbled. "Any energy spikes?"

"Only a small one that could have been attributed to asteroids colliding." Fox returned. "Do you really think that Zakicowi would have left something powered?"

"If he thought he was coming back soon enough." Sonnet answered. "Or if he was that confident that this area wouldn't be touched. For that matter, he could have left some passive systems on, simply because he was worried about damage due to other asteroids."

That last part was the one that made the most sense to Pruit. He would certainly want a hyper-cable setup to alert him should his prize be moved or damaged. And that would require quite a few systems to remain up and running.

"Make for it." Curzo called out, as he walked back toward the command chair.

"Aye captain." Replied a crewman who had come up to help fill out the bridge stations. He was, at present, acting at helmsman. He was a good solid lad, but inexperienced with this particular ship. Most ship designs were similar but often just different enough that old habits could result in some interesting mistakes.

"ETA?" Curzo demanded.

"Five hours." The helmsman replied.

"Very well." Curzo was visibly disappointed. Still, it was five hours to relax. He just secretly wished that Sonnet wasn't with him. He could then spend some time using that human slave as a distraction. With Sonnet onboard, and her obvious protective streak where that little female was concerned, such an attempt was out of the question. So, he would do the next best thing and get himself a drink. Perhaps even a nap would be in order.

"Keep me apprised." He ordered as he strode off the bridge and toward his captain's quarters.

"AYE Sir!" Was the last then he heard as he cleared the bridge into the hallway.

CHAPTER 29

"Course projection puts them on intercept. ETA five hours." Green announced as she looked over her scans. "Looks like you called it on the money."

"I wouldn't break my arm patting myself on the back just yet." Wyatt drawled. "There's still a heap that could go wrong with this little endeavor. But Curzo is a straight forward kind of fellow. He's more than likely going to come plowing in, just straight on towards us, and try to get to get his hands on the prize as soon as possible. That should play right into our plan."

"What's the backup plan?" She gave him a look that was suspicious.

"Run, shoot, hide, and try not to die." Wyatt replied. "Once we engage in this field, we're committed. There is too much debris to try and go to hyper and we'd never make it to the limit anyway. We might be able to shake them in the field, especially since we can absorb so many more heavy hits than he can. But I still wouldn't like our odds."

"What would you say the odds are of your primary plan working?" Green asked cautiously.

"About seventy/thirty against." He sighed in reply. He then, reached into his pocket and pulled out his star. He held it up, turned it over in his hands and just looked at it for a minute. When he was finished, he reached into his vest and reattached the star back where it rightfully belonged.

"Well." She began as she started walking toward him, throwing a little extra sway in her hips as she walked. "If we're bound and determined to go down fighting, I want to go down satisfied as well."

Wyatt gave her a suspicious but appreciative eye as she stood before his command chair.

"What exactly did you have in mind, little lady?" He inquired, as returned her hungry look.

"We have five hours to kill." She then pulled the zipper on her flight suit and let it fall away, revealing a body that was definitely worth a second, or even third, look.

"Well, I can't imagine a more pleasant way to spend the time." Wyatt rose from his chair and the two shared one of the most passionate, and sober exchanges the two had undertaken in a long time.

****

Kenjay was making his way slowly through the passages behind the walls, but was not finding it very accommodating. Because of that fact, he always made sure he went last, whenever they used the secret conveyance. Just in case he got stuck, the two youths could continue on and escape. Getting caught that way, or possibly killed, wasn't the glorious death that he would have imagined for himself, but still, dying for someone else to have a chance at life, was still honorable. Kenjay, however, would not like his death plague to indicate that he died because he ate too much. Although, dying because one was too fat to fit down a passageway, was one sure way to be sure that his death would be remembered.

"I do not wish to doubt you small one." Kenjay whispered to his protégé. "But are you sure this passage will take us to the engine room? We seem to be going the wrong way."

"This passage will not." Oso admitted, but continued on before his teacher could object. "We must make a change at the medical bay. We will be exposed while we transition from one passage to the next. But there should be no one there."

Kenjay was a trifle irked that the lad had left out this rather important detail, but he knew it wouldn't have made a difference. Even with that bit of information he still would have made the decision to proceed with their plan.

The plan was simple. Place a remote switch that would short circuit the engine's control computers and the engines would automatically shut down. Even someone as ship illiterate as Kenjay was, knew that modern ship propulsion relied heavily on the computer. Shut it down, and you shut everything down. The only problem had been learning the correct spot to place their remote sabotage device. Turned out that engineering schematics were plentiful in the computer files. It had evidently been something that Oso was required to learn, but had not been dutifully studying.

The device itself, had been simple to construct with what they had readily available. Oso had several remote controlled, motorized toys that were easily accessible. It was a simple matter to disassemble one, replace a drive wheel with a sharpened disc and connect it to the remote and a power source. The only question was, would the remote have the power and range to transmit and receive through several hundred feet of ship. That was something no one could answer and their one great gamble.

There was also the matter of when to use the device. If Wyatt truly was deceased and never made an appearance then it became a matter of trusting the pirates to keep their word to him. Then the device would only be triggered if it looked like they were in danger. If Wyatt did find a way to ride to the rescue, then Kenjay would trigger the device, figuring that a disabled ship would be much easier to capture.

"Forgive me for inquiring at this late date." Kenjay whispered to Oso. "But do these secret passages, not compromise the ability of the ship to compartmentalize in the event of the loss of pressure?"

"Very much so." Oso admitted. "Father was more concerned with boarders than he was ship to ship combat. For that we always wore environmental suits and depressurized the hull before combat. Father thought it would help contain any ship damage if there was no oxygen to fuel fires or pressure to blow things apart."

Kenjay nodded in understanding and limited approval of the strategy. The truth of the matter was that ships preparing to fight each other, often had one another within sensor range for hours before the first shots were fired, so there would be plenty of time to prepare for combat. It was extremely rare for one ship to sneak up on another. Even the best cloaking devices left sensor shadows. Also ships small enough to be cloaked, were not used very much in combat operations as they were usually too light to be of any real value. One would occasionally hear tales of a small ship sneaking up on a larger one and planting a limpet mine or even ramming it while packed with explosive, but they were few, far between and usually the sign of a desperation. Any ship and crew that attempted such a thing tended to die very quickly.

"Are we almost there?" Annwyl looked back and asked Oso. Her face was dripping with sweat and her breathing rapid. It was clear that she was fighting her fear of small places. She wouldn't have come if she wasn't vital to the plan and for the fact that she wouldn't be able to live with herself in anything happened to her friends while she was safe in her quarters.

"Just a few more minutes." Oso returned, in a voice as calm and reassuring as he could make it. It was clear that he was beginning to become concerned with Annwyl's well-being. This was a big step for the selfish boy that just a few weeks ago, who was concerned for no one but himself.

True to his word, they approached the secret hatch in the medical bay just a few minutes later. Once there, Oso pressed his ear to the panel and listened as well as he could. After several moments of hearing nothing, he quietly pushed the panel out of place and slid it to the side. He then exited the secret passage and immediately found himself standing between two sleeping crewmembers, who had chosen the medical bay to be their quarters.

He motioned for the others to be quiet, not that they weren't already. He then took Annwyl's hand and led her across the room to the panel on the other side. Kenjay, meanwhile, stealthily pushed the panel they had just come through, back into place, leaving no trace of their presence behind.

For a moment, the sword master stared at one of the blasters the men had laid on the table. Grabbing it would be a simply procedure and it might come in handy later. But the thought of what could happen if a crewmember realized, and he surly would realize it in short order, that his weapon was missing, quickly changed his mind.

Instead he crept over to where the two young ones were waiting, and joined them in the secret passageway. After silently moving the panel back into place, they continued on their journey toward the engine room.

****

Four hours and thirty minutes after leaving the bridge, and enjoying a much needed and refreshing nap, the pirate captain returned to his duty station.

"Status update!" Curzo demanded as he stormed onto the command deck.

"On course and on schedule." A crewman called out from his position at the navigation table. "We are thirty minutes to intercept."

"Begin slowing for zero/zero intercept at ten-thousand clicks from the target." The captain barked.

That intercept would put the *Revenge* completely stationary, relative to the movement of the asteroid containing his quarry. A perfect position from which to begin salvage operations. That was, if he still had a construction pod. Still it would be easy to move into a docking configuration from that stance, and if it turned out that operations couldn't be carried out without more equipment, it was a good position to take all the surveys needed for a legal claim. Not that Curzo could show his face to make that kind of claim, but Sonnet certainly could. As far as the rest of the galaxy was concerned, she was still and honest, upstanding citizen. Following in the footsteps of her famous father, as an explorer and salvager.

"Beginning to slow for zero/zero intercept ten-thousand clicks from the target." The crewman responded in a professional voice that Curzo didn't really expect. Still, a lot of the crew he had taken on over the years, had been former navy and still reverted to those professional protocols. Curzo didn't really care for the call backs of commands, his crew sometimes sounding like a drunken parrot, but even he would have to admit that it had helped catch some bad communication when passing orders, in the past.

"Now we sit and wait." Curzo mused.

CHAPTER 30

"They're slowing." Green announced from her station at the nav and helm positions. "Estimated zero/zero intercept at thirty-five minutes. That's if they go for docking."

"I'm not going to count on them coming in straight for a docking procedure." Wyatt explained. "Although that would be ideal. No, I'm betting he's going to take the simple precaution of taking a survey of the wreck first. At which point we would be screwed if we simply sat still. Which we won't."

"Orders?" Green bit her lip in anticipation. She was a combination of nervous energy and calm professionalism. Sure, she was afraid, as she always was before and engagement, but she could control her fear and not let in rule her decisions. That was what was truly brave about her.

Wyatt made some quick calculations, first in his head, then he backed himself up with the computer. He then made the course he estimated that they enemy would take appear on the main screen.

"If I'm correct in my calculations about what Curzo is going to do," He put that tiny, little qualifier on his strategy. "He'll make for a point about here." He then made a target appear, where he believed Curzo would stop to do his survey. "So that would make his point of commitment to be approximately, here." He then made another target spot appear in a different color than the first. "As soon as he crosses that point, that's his Rubicon. He's going to be committed on that course. He won't be able to bring up power fast enough to make a difference. If we start out when he gets there, we'll meet him in the middle. Hopefully this old girl will hold together."

Green smiled as she lovingly patted the wall next to her. She really liked the ship, regardless of the creepy cargo they were hauling around at the moment.

What they were doing was technically illegal. Any alien technology, of a previously unknown or uncontacted species, was to be turned over to the Interplanetary Space Corps. That way they could gage the technological level of any potential threats and learn all they could about them. Punishments for withholding alien tech could get severe, and included death by hanging as it was interpreted to be a form of treason. The fact that Wyatt was a Marshal, muddied the water a little bit, as he was authorized to bend and even break a few laws in the pursuit of his duties. It would be as stretch, to say that his ignoring of the law would include a violation of the highest order, but the fact that hostages and children were involved, could go a long way toward swaying opinion on the subject.

There was also the fact that Wyatt would be within his rights to take possession of any alien artifacts discovered, as long as he was intending on turning them over to the proper authority at the earliest moment possible. That clearly fell into a law enforcement duty.

"How are we on offensive capability?" Green knew that Wyatt had been studying all he could about his new alien ship, but weaponry was not in great supply onboard.

"As for the ship, if this tub has any offensive lasers or missiles, I've yet to find them." He grumped. "As for boring lasers and grapplers, I think we'll be in good shape. If we can latch onto his hull, we can cut our way inside easily. Once we are inside, it could get sticky in a hurry. The blasters we had brought with us, only have two shots remaining apiece. I haven't found any internal small arms armory either. But I did find one pretty powerful laser, that looks like it was used for cutting rock. I did a range test on it, and it cut through a bulkhead at fifty feet. Not the lightest thing around, I have to use a shoulder strap and fire from my hip, but that's not a problem."

"That means you'll have to expose a lot of yourself to use it." Green pointed out correctly.

"Can't be helped." He replied flatly. "Let's just hope we don't get ourselves killed, before we get a chance to get ourselves killed."

****

Kenjay emerged from the panel into the engine room, close on the heels of the two youths. He then proceeded to try and make himself as small as possible, as they did not exit the secret passage at a point of concealment. Rather they had to ingloriously slide onto a walkway from a point slightly above it. It was not a stealthy maneuver to be sure.

"I do wish we were rather less exposed." Kenjay quipped as he looked around to make sure they were not seen.

"Couldn't be helped." Oso explained. "Putting the passageway in a spot where it would be completely concealed would have compromised the frame integrity of the ship. Father was only going to go so far when it came to compromising safety."

"The engine room seems deserted except for one man by the main console." Kenjay observed. "Which is, unfortunately, the only console we are interested in at the moment."

"Is it time for me to go distract him." Annwyl offered, as she looked down at the man.

"How?" Oso gave her a questioning look.

"The same way I used to distract your father." She replied, to which he paled slightly.

Originally that was what Kenjay intended from the start. Which was why she was essential to his plan. Now, looking at the girl and thinking about what she had already endured, his blood boiled and he changed his mind.

"I will not let you degrade yourself like that." Kenjay informed her, in a sharp whisper. "We will simply find another way."

"He used my body as a toy." She shot back. "I will use it as a weapon."

"I believe that will be unnecessary." Oso replied, and they all watched in horror as he picked up a pipe that was laying on the catwalk and dropped it over the railing.

The pipe tumbled as it fell, but it's aim was true. I landed perpendicular to the man sitting at the console, making a hollow clanking noise as it contacted his head. The man then slumped to the floor as if he were melting.

"Excellent shot." Kenjay complimented. "But this might just give us away."

"Possible." Oso agreed as he looked at his master. "Then again, the pipe was already up here. Hopefully they will interpret this as an accident."

"Let us hope so."

The trio then made their way down to the main engineering console, checked the crewman and found that he had indeed expired, and then they got to work.

Thirty minutes later the trio were walking down the main hallway, like nothing had ever happened. Most of the crew were so used to seeing Kenjay walking around free that no one asked them any questions. They then made their way to the main cargo hold for a practice session for Oso in his hand to hand training. Something that Kenjay had asked to continue and had been granted permission to do so. Sonnet was familiar with his routine, which started long before she took over the ship. She saw no reason to discontinue it.

"Master Kenjay." Oso huffed between strikes as he recoiled from his teacher. "When do you think we'll have to make our move?"

"Hopefully never." Kenjay replied, his own heartrate elevated with the exertion, not that he would let it show. "The wise warrior...?"

"Seeks only to be prepared to fight." Oso finished the ancient quote. "But seeks to avoid battle whenever possible."

"Correct." The older alien nodded in approval. "We will hope that everything will play out equitably and there will be no need to execute our plan. But we will be prepared, in the event that all parties involved do not wish for things to end peacefully."

"If you desire peace…?" Annwyl interjected.

"Prepare for war." Oso finished.

****

"Captain." The crewman at the scanner array called out to Curzo. "I'm getting some strange readings here."

"Specify." Sonnet barked, over stepping Curzo, which earned her a look from the angry samurai.

"Uh…The ship we are reading, does not comply to the Wells Argo stage, the *Western Rose.*" The crewman continued, shooting an apologetic look at his captain. "In fact, the ship we are reading doesn't match any known vessel."

"What about size?" Sonnet demanded. "Mass? Does it come close to the ship we are looking for in any category?"

"Size and mass aren't too far off." The crewman indicated, as he put his readings up on the main view so his captain could see what he was talking about. "But the configuration, hull design and even the composite material, don't match the *Rose.*"

"Could Zakicowi have camouflaged the ship to look like something else?" Curzo rubbed his chin in thought.

"It's possible to make a ship like that look like something else." Sonnet confirmed. "Enough reflective webbing can make something disappear. But why make it look like another ship? Why not make it look like rock? Like just part of the asteroid?"

"Reduce speed." Curzo called out. "Bring us in slower. I don't like this."

"May I remind you that our time here is not unlimited." Sonnet jabbed at the alien, who was basically her flag captain.

"You may remind me." Cruzo returned. "Once!"

At that, Sonnet chose to remain silent. It would do good for her to remind herself that she was outnumbered by a crew that was loyal to their captain. As much as he might enjoy the profitability of working with her, she was not the end all of his existence. Basically, she was expendable, especially after they got their hands on the booty. If there was truly enough there to retire happily, her usefulness to him was at an end. She decided that she had better stick closer to Fox Pruit. He might just turn out to be her best chance of survival if things went south.

CHAPTER 31

"They're slowing." Wyatt grumbled as he looked at the view screen. "That's going to move the point of no return too close to us. They're not going to make it."

"Orders captain?" Green replied, with a defiance in her voice that would have steeled any man's resolve.

"Give me the best speed you can muster, mister!" We're taking this fight to them. "Time for this old girl to join the dance."

There was no doubt in Wyatt's mind that Green was pushing this ancient ship well past its designed safety parameters, but he wasn't going to say anything to her about it. Truth was that he was mad enough and determined enough that he would have done the same thing.

Still the ship creaked and groaned as it departed the asteroid and made both pilots take a good look at each other, concern, and maybe a little doubt, etched upon their faces. But neither made a move or command to reduce speed. It was time to go hell bent for leather and they both knew it.

Wyatt then punched in a broadcast frequency into the coms unit and prepared to transmit. He had something special in mind for Curzo. He only hoped his plan worked.

****

"The ship is moving." The crewman at the scanner console called out as he double checked his readings and confirmed what he was seeing.

Curzo thought about ordering the man to check again, but he knew he wouldn't have called it out without being sure. He was a good and reliable, longtime member of his crew, despite having to deal with the handicap of being born a human.

"Course and speed?" Curzo called out.

"Collision course!" The man replied, and never got a chance to call out the speed before Curzo cut him off.

"Bring us about." Curzo yelled out. "Show them our broadside. All quarters clear for action!"

The Revenge pivoted beautifully. Whatever else could be said about Curzo as a pirate, captain, or dishonored alien, he was an excellent ship handler and his crew was well drilled. Ports were cleared, air tight compartments were sealed, and guns were run out at a speed that would make any professional naval man envious.

"Time to optimal range?" Curzo called out to the crewman glued to his scanner.

"Two minutes." He called back.

"Captain!" Fox Pruit's voice came loudly from the coms.

"Report." Curzo didn't bother to berate the man for interrupting his ship in combat. He knew Fox well enough to know that the man didn't speak unless it was important, and if he was interrupting now the information he had must be downright catastrophic.

"The crew are reporting step down transformers in all of the ship's energy weapons." Fox announced, in voice that was clearly concerned.

"Of course." Curzo grumbled. "That meddlesome marshal didn't remove the guns he simply stepped them down to a legal power rating.

"How long to remove them?" He then demanded.

"Three minutes." Fox returned.

"Remove the ones on the opposite battery first." Curzo ordered him, surprisingly. "I don't want to risk not getting the first broadside off, and a low power shot is better than no shot."

"Aye aye captain." Fox replied, shutting off the com link and getting to work.

"After we let fly the first broadside, roll our back to them." Curzo ordered. "He doesn't really want to collide with us, not with his friends on board. He'll probably shoot over the top of us, so we'll put her into a slow spin and fire as we bear."

"Aye sir." Replied his helmsman as he started calculating thrust for the maneuver they had executed taking on other ships in the past.

All the captain could do now was wait for optimal range. Just a few more seconds.

****

"Master!" Oso called out to his teacher as alarms began to blare and crew began to move about in a scurry. "That alarm is for battle stations. I would recognize it anywhere."

"Then perhaps we will get the opportunity to put our little surprise into practice a little sooner than we believed. I also suspect that we should make our way to your quarters and retrieve our other little distractions." He didn't want to use the word *weapons*, just in case anyone was listening. Not that he thought anyone would have wasted the energy doing that, but he wanted to be cautious. Curzo was not a forgiving sort, if he thought Kenjay was conspiring against him he wouldn't hesitate to kill him. Even orders from Sonnet wouldn't be able to save him.

CHAPTER 32

"We are moving as fast as I can get her up do in our restricted distance. In other words maximum acceleration has been achieved." Green called out as she finished sealing up her environmental suit. "Impact in thirty seconds."

"Let's just hope he doesn't figure out what we're doing." Wyatt mumbled. "Time to optimal range?"

"ten seconds." She replied.

"Then here goes nothing." Wyatt hit the transmit button and sent a signal to the *Revenge*. He could only the envision the panic that would be induced on the bridge if it worked out the way he planned.

****

"Captain! All weapons are offline." He gunner called out from his station on the bridge.

"What?" Curzo leapt to his feet and stormed over behind the man. "How?"

"Best guess is he had a command in his gunnery computer to kill the guns if he broadcast on a certain frequency." The gunner explained, as he guessed correctly. "We received a transmission from that ship just before the guns went offline."

"Take us up." Curzo shouted at his helmsman. "Straight up twenty-thousand-meters."

The helmsman complied immediately and probably saved the ship from being impaled but Wyatt's vessel.

The ship lurched slightly and everyone had the feeling of getting pushed down into their shoes for a moment, until the inertial dampeners could catch up.

"Rolling on lateral axis." The helmsman then called out as he executed the previous order and rolled the ship to bring the other broadside to bear.

"Can you countermand his deactivation command?" Curzo yelled to his gunner.

"Already have." He replied with a smile. "Firing."

****

Wyatt and Green were tossed slightly by the impact from the shots from their opponent. The shots were more powerful than they expected, but their ship was massive and well armored.

"Well I guess they found the stepdown transformers." Wyatt grumped.

"They are going up and over us as well." Green griped as she attempted to bring the cutting lasers to bear and failed. "Looks like it's going to be cat and mouse from here."

"Well that's not good." He replied absently as he looked over his board to try and find anything that would help them. "I didn't expect them to be able to react so quickly. I guess this Curzo's reputation is well deserved."

"Well," Green shrugged. "It's been nice knowing you."

"We're not dead yet." He gave her a hungry grin. "Not by a long shot."

****

"I believe that now would be the most opportune moment." Kenjay called out to his two roommates. "We had all best steel ourselves. I have the feeling that it will not take them long to realize that we are to blame for what is about to happen."

Annwyl and Oso both nodded in response. He then pushed the button on the transmitter and everything went black.

****

If anyone could have seen the captain, they would have surely described his face as a combination of shock and fury. It was, perhaps, fortunate that it was too dark to see him.

"Status report." Curzo called out, as emergency lights began to flicker on. "What the hell is going on?"

"Instruments indicated that the main engine control computer is down." His scanner replied. "We've lost all power from the mains. The backups are spinning up, but they won't give us engine power. We're down to maneuvering thrusters, life support and some other necessary functions. I've been trying to contact engineering, but haven't gotten a reply."

"So we're dead in the water." Curzo spat.

It was then that Sonnet stormed onto the bridge. Her look said it all. A combination of fear, fury and confusion. She didn't even get a chance to ask the question in her mind before Curzo informed her what had probably happened.

"I'm willing to bet that this is your business partner's doing." Curzo spat. "I should have killed him before you brought this colossal failure upon us."

She shot him a look that should have sent daggers flying from her eyes. Instead he simply reached over and drew his sword from the scabbard next to his command chair. He then paused for a moment, and grabbed a second sword. The one that properly belonged to Master Kenjay.

"Get two men to engineering to effect repairs." Curzo ordered. "The rest of you prepare to repel boarders. And our guests are now to be regarded as hostiles."

Men got up and scrambled to get weapons. Curzo and Sonnet also strode out to meet their opponents head on.

CHAPTER 33

"Wyatt!" Green yelled in disbelief as she couldn't understand why she was seeing what she was. "The *Revenge*, she's gone dead. Scanners show total power down."

"What?" He then called up his own scans and likewise studied them with the same incredulous look. "What the hell just happened? On second thought, who cares. Put us on course to grapple the cargo hold. It will be our best bet to get in with some cover."

"On it." She shouted back.

It only took minutes to position the ship to grab hold of the Revenge and punch through her hull right at the cargo hold airlock. All seal readings read in the green as they effectively had 'docked' with the other ship. The only problem now, was the time it was going to take them to get to the exit of the ship and engage the enemy. That delay was going to give the enemy plenty of time to get ready. Still, it was necessary.

"How many of them are there?" Green asked nervously as she checked her blaster for the hundredth time.

"I'm guessing here, but I'm figuring about fifteen." Wyatt replied. "Curzo, Sonnet, Fox and twelve crew."

"And we have four shots, a mining laser and our attitudes?" Green listed with a nervous chuckle.

"Don't underestimate attitude." Wyatt replied with a lopsided grin. "Hell hath no fury, but woman scorn, except a man betrayed."

They then opened the hatch and stormed out into the cargo hold, to face their fate.

****

Kenjay and Oso were back to back in the dimly lit hallway. Two crewmen, who originally had been heading to engineering, already tried to incept them, not realizing that they were now armed and acting against them. They now lay bleeding to death on the deck.

"Where to now?" Oso asked as he wiped the blood from his father's blade.

"We make our way to the cargo hold." Kenjay replied, breathing a little heavier than he should be. He guessed that this was a trifle more adrenaline than he had bargained for. He had trained for many years, and was a sword master of the ninth degree, but he had never, until this moment, taken another life before. He was quite the student of training to fight, so that one wouldn't have to fight.

Fortunately, they made sure to take the blasters and extra charge packs from the two dispatched crewmen and started down the passageway toward the cargo hold.

"Why there?" Annwyl whispered.

"It would be the most logical place for a boarding party to attempt to gain entry." Kenjay replied quietly. "I have been studying ship to ship attacks while we have been confined to Oso's quarters. The hold is usually the place where ships are boarded, mostly because it takes up so much space, there is usually more cover, and it is often where the goods pirates are trying to steal are located in the first place.

"Makes sense." Annwyl conceded as she flipped a knife over in her hand and sent it flying down the hallway, striking a crewman who had just rounded the corner. Fortunately for her, the crewmember was human and her blade sank deep into his chest. He slumped to the deck in a gasp and moan.

"Excellent throw." Kenjay complimented the former slave girl.

"Thank you." She returned. She did not bother to retrieve her knife, she had others, and he was too far the wrong direction. She briefly considered running and grabbing his blaster, but she was unfamiliar with how to use them and knew that neither Kenjay or Oso were comfortable with them either. If they could reach Wyatt, who she assumed was the cause of all this commotion, they could get him a blaster to use and that was paramount. She also suspected that if the time came that she was forced to use one, there would probably be plenty of them laying around.

Kenjay's head shot up as he heard several crewmembers heading their way. "Hide!" He whispered.

Oso quickly grabbed the two and dragged them over to a place of concealment. He had grown up on this ship and knew every nook and cranny. If anyone could get about undetected, it was him.

****

"Our hull has been breached!" Curzo shouted to any crew that might not have gotten the point, as he and the others made their way toward the cargo hold, to join in the fracas.

Fox checked his blaster, adjusted his Neo-Stetson hat and followed at a more leisurely pace. He wasn't excited about getting into a firefight with Wyatt Toranado. Even though there was a part of him that was itching for an excuse to find out which one of them was the best, or at least better. He had come to the conclusion that there was no such thing as the best, when it came to his profession. Someone was always better, or luckier. Now did not seem to be the most opportune moment to find out that Wyatt was simply lucky, as he had learned the hard way, that luck almost always trumps skill.

Cruzo and several of his crew entered into the cargo bay and took up defensive positions. From what he was seeing, there was only one way for the boarders to enter. Straight through the cargo bay airlock. There was cover off to the sides of the doorway, but they wouldn't be able to stay hidden for long. A long-protracted battle favored him and his crew, not the duo of Green and Wyatt.

He took a moment to study the vessel he was seeing. It was unlike anything he had seen before. The front seemed to open like a bird's beak, with a ramp coming down out of it. It seemed to penetrate and seal, which could be very useful in a pirate's line of work. He would no longer have to rely on using only a docking point, or penetrating a hull and having to fight in environmental suits. Whatever kind of vessel this was, he wanted it.

"Stand ready." Curzo growled to his crew. "We make our stand here."

****

"Master." Oso whispered to Kenjay as they made their way toward the cargo bay. "They are all waiting for Wyatt."

"In this position, it does not look good for our marshal." Annwyl observed.

"We may need to provide him some kind of distraction." Kenjay looked around in vain to find something that he could throw, or drop in order to distract the crew. But he saw nothing that would accomplish the desired results without exposing him to lethal fire. And as much as Kenjay liked Wyatt, Kenjay was Kenjay's favorite person.

****

Wyatt and Green were positioned just inside the ramp to their newly acquired ship. Both of them were breathing heavy already, and neither looked particularly ready to run down the ramp and engage a superior enemy.

"Any ideas?" Green asked, ever hopeful.

"Just one." Wyatt replied as he studied a control panel. "This ship is designed to burrow into a solid surface, seal up, and allow for mining operations, right?"

Green simply shrugged and then nodded in reply.

"Well it would stand to reason that the operators would want the crew to start to work as quickly as possible. So if everything is hot after it burrows in, I'm thinking there must be a mechanism here that will cool it down." Wyatt then called up a screen and found what he was looking for. "Ah! Here it is. Liquid nitrogen, and a lot of it."

He then manipulated multiple controls and looked over at his cohort.

"Get ready." The smile on his face said it all. He was going to eat the enemy alive.

Wyatt activated the control and huge clouds of fog, in the form of rapidly expanding nitrogen, rolled forward. The hissing sound was deafening and many of Curzo's crew flinched and some even reached up to cover their ears. A few wild shots rang out as a couple crew members fired at where they thought the boarders would appear, even though they could see nothing.

Curzo cursed as he watched the fog roll forward, engulfing the cargo hold in a dense cloud that was nearly impenetrable.

Kenjay saw the fog as well, and smiled as he realized that his friend needed no help from him creating a distraction. He then surged forward and attacked the surprised crewmen from behind.

Wyatt and Green surged down the ramp, and immediately moved away from the airlock hatch. Blaster bolts sizzled by, barely missing them despite their owner's blind aim. Wyatt took stock of where they were coming from, however, and let loose with the mining laser he had strapped over his shoulder. The blinding flash of the beam was reflected and seemingly magnified by the fog. There was then a satisfying explosion and scream as the laser blasted apart a hover bike that a crewman was cowering behind. He would no longer be a threat.

"FALL BACK!" Curzo yelled, as he realized he had lost the initiative. "We'll take them in the passageway."

He then turned to head that direction when he caught sight of Kenjay and Oso, attacking, hacking and killing his men from the rear. Three men went down in seconds as Kenjay masterfully whirled in a deadly dance of precision and steel.

Fox, who was slightly behind Curzo, also saw the sword master in action and decided he was not someone he wanted to come into reach of. Instead he aimed and fired a shot that would certainly end the warrior alien.

Kenjay turned and saw the flash from Fox's blaster. He then moved his blade with amazing speed and precision. Unfortunately, the metal of Kenjay's blade was not designed for what he was attempting and the blaster bolt burned through it and struck Kenjay in the chest. The sword master went down in a heap.

Green had expended her two shots, which had resulted in one less crewman being available to Curzo. She then scrambled forward to try and retrieve a weapon of any sort. She knew where the one she had shot had gone down, but didn't know the exact location of the ones Wyatt had killed. She finally rounded the crate that the man had been using for cover, only to realize that his blaster was gone.

"Looking for something?" Came the familiar voice of Sonnet as she held up the deceased pirate's weapon.

"Well I was hoping." Green sighed as she stood up and faced her former employer.

"It is a shame." Sonnet frowned. "I had brought you onboard, hoping you could be persuaded to join our team. I could have used a talent like yours. Not to mention you were one of the few that had the credentials Wyatt would have accepted and skill that might be needed.

"But the more I watched you, the more I came to realize that you would never betray a contract, or Wyatt for that matter. It looks like my degree in psychology has been useful after all."

"Well, I'm happy to disappoint you." Green spat.

"Consider this the termination of your employment." Sonnet mocked, she then squeezed the firing stud and sent a bolt of white hot energy straight through Green's chest.

Wyatt turned the corner of one of the crates, only to send two more bad guys off to the great beyond, courtesy of his mining laser. It was then that it let off a shower of sparks and ceased to function.

"Well that was fun while it lasted." Wyatt then dropped the useless piece of equipment and made his way over to the two crew he had dispatched. Once there he recovered one of the blasters and, after checking it, slipped it into his still present holster. He made sure to take extra ammunition packs as well, as looked around at the now diminishing fog and pondered his next move.

Kenjay had never experienced pain like that which was burning through him at the moment. His chest seemed to be on fire, which was appropriate considering the burns he had suffered. His breathing was labored and his eyes watered from the pain. He looked down at his still smoking chest and then at his blown in half sword, and reasoned that enough energy from the blaster bolt had spent itself on the blade, that the hit he received was not immediately fatal.

He struggled to his feet, and looked around for Annwyl and Oso. He did not immediately see them, nor did he know where they had gone off to. He did not know that they had run the only direction available to them. They had gone up one of the ship's ladders.

"So you still live." Curzo growled, as he approached the wounded sword master. "Let us see if we can correct that condition."

Kenjay turned and faced the pirate. His vision was settling, but his entire body felt heavy and unresponsive. He knew this wasn't going to end well.

"I'm afraid you have me at a disadvantage." Kenjay held his arms out to his side. "As you can see, I no longer have any weapons."

"Then perhaps you would like this." Curzo held up Kenjay's own sword. The one he had taken from him earlier. He then tossed to the wounded swordsman. "Never let it be said, that Curzo allowed a brother to die without honor."

Kenjay took a moment and slowly drew his blade from its scabbard. He then lovingly turned it over in his hand and once again marveled at its construction and beauty. It seemed funny to him, the things he was noticing now that he was about to die.

CHAPTER 34

Sonnet had met up with another crewman and made her way over toward the alien ship. She searched the thinning fog for her partner, Fox, but to no avail. She knew he had to be close, but where, exactly, eluded her. She would simply have to hope that he had the same idea that she had, as she disappeared up the ramp into the foreign vessel.

Fox had spent as much time ducking and moving as he had shooting and missing. He knew Wyatt was close, he could almost feel the man breathing down his neck. Still he couldn't get into position to get a shot off. At least not an aimed one. It was frustrating that such a good marksman should not be able to set up for a killing shot, because his prey was so quick and good at remaining under cover.

Soon he reached the conclusion that he needed to worry more about escape than about killing a single man. With that in mind he started working his way back toward the alien ship with the idea of using it to get away. The problem was going to be piloting it. Although trained as a Fox had no interest in keeping up his piloting skills in the past, now that oversight was going to be a problem for him. Still, he had spent enough time aboard ship that he wasn't inept when it came to being proficient at their operation. He just hoped that the alien ship was advanced enough that it was *easy* to fly.

He knew Sonnet was well versed in piloting, although she didn't have a rating and it was a fact that she hid well. The problem was that he didn't know where she was, or if she was even alive. He just had to hope that she had the good sense to make for the obvious escape route. Just like he was now.

It turned out, that his goal was a little too obvious.

"Hold it right there, Fox." Wyatt drawled, as he stepped out from behind a crate, directly behind his fellow bounty hunter and hired gun.

Fox froze. He wasn't sure of Wyatt's exact location, nor did he think he would have been fast enough to turn, aim and fire, before the marshal could cut him down.

"Well it looks like you got the drop on me marshal." Fox acknowledged as he slowly turned around, his hands raised. Even though he still held his blaster in one of them. He then gave Wyatt an evil look. The kind that rips right through a man's soul. The same kind that Wyatt was giving him. "What do you say Wyatt? Do you want to find out once and for all who's better?" Fox slid his blaster into his holster, and gave Wyatt a chilling, almost insane look.

Wyatt, likewise, holstered his blaster. The two then stood there. Each one waiting for that one blink, one look, one motion that would signal the contest was beginning. The high noon showdown had begun. The question was, which one would be quick and which one would be dead.

Kenjay felt energized by his sword. He knew it was only in his head, but still the rush of power surged through him. He drew himself up, and held his sword ready.

"Let's finish this." Curzo growled as he lunged at his opponent.

Kenjay blocked Curzo's first strike easily enough. He was twice the sword handler the pirate was. At least he would be at full health. In his current condition he was dubious, and with good reason.

Attacks, blocks, parries and ripostes became the order of the day. Each one moving, and swinging, trying to find an opening and work through their opponent's defenses. Normally Kenjay would have made short work of the pirate, but his condition was anything but normal. He received cut after cut from his alien brethren. Nothing deep, but still distracting, as if his burning chest wasn't problematic enough.

Curzo was not having it all his own way either. He had thought that he would be able to defeat the injured sword master, only to find out that was far from the truth. He too, received blow after blow, and his blood flowed and soaked his armor. He wasn't hurt badly, yet, but he soon reached the conclusion that he wasn't going to win this battle, so he shifted tactics to try and outlast his adversary. If only he could stay alive, until Kenjay succumb to his injuries, he would win the day.

His strategy seemed to be paying dividends as Kenjay stumbled, time and again. Barely making it back to deflect or block strikes from Curzo. His vision was fading, his head throbbing and his chest was in agony.

Finally, he stepped back, unable to press another attack. It would seem, that the sword master would have to concede that he couldn't defeat this ruffian. It was then that fate intervened.

"Heads up!" Came a yell from up above, on the catwalk that bisected the upper level of the cargo hold.

Both swordsmen looked up, just in time to see Oso plummeting downward. His father's blade in his hands, and in full swing. His timing was perfect as he brought the sword down on top of Curzo's skull. Slicing deeply amid the harsh crunching of bone and splattering of blood.

Curzo couldn't understand why he suddenly couldn't move. His thoughts were now jumbled and confused. Surely, he had beaten the sword master. There couldn't be any doubt about that. Why then, did he feel tired. Those thoughts continued as his body fell backward, smashing to the deck with a deafening clatter of armor. His blood flowed freely, staining the deck a bright crimson. As he looked up, he noticed one of the lights on the ceiling was out and a last disconnected thought crawled through his damaged brain. *I'll have to get someone to fix that.* Then, darkness took him. And the mighty Curzo, scourge of space, was no more.

"Don't even tell me that there was no honor in that." Oso grumbled at his teacher as he retrieved his blade and went over to assist the wounded friend.

"I wouldn't dream of it." Kenjay replied with a chuckle. With that he slumped to the deck.

"So what's it going to be Wyatt?" Fox again taunted the marshal. "You gonna make a play, or am I just going to turn and walk away?"

Wyatt looked the man he knew as Fox Pruit, up and down. He then nodded at the fellow bounty hunter and grinned.

"You're not in my contract." Wyatt replied with a chuckle.

"I thought not." Fox then turned and started toward the alien ship. "Maybe some other time."

He then disappeared up the ramp and beak like entry started to close.

"Probably not." Wyatt replied quietly as he watched the entryway of the alien ship slowly close.

Wyatt then rushed over to the airlock seal and pressed it. Closing the hatch and sealing off the breached section of the hull from the main hold. He then watched through the airlock porthole as the alien ship backed away, metal tearing and atmosphere blowing out into space.

After watching empty space for what seemed like an eternity, Wyatt finally turned and went to find his friends. If they were still alive.

CHAPTER 35

Wyatt helped Annwyl and Oso get Kenjay to the medical bay. He swore bitterly the entire way about Green not making it. It was better that he had not known before, if he had, he would have surely taken Fox up on his duel, if only out of anguish and anger.

Once at the sickbay Annwyl, who seemed very adept at patching the alien anatomy got to work. It would seem that she had performed this type of function on Zakicowi many times, so she knew a little bit about what she was doing.

Wyatt was then filled in on what had happened to disable his ship, by Oso, so he made his way up to the bridge to see if he could run the engineering scans from there, and survey the damage. He really wanted to go to engineering and start fixing it, but there was still a hostile ship out there, and he wanted to see if he could find out what was going on.

When he arrived on the bridge he found that most of the AUX systems had come online. Backup power was taking over, but the engines were still non-functional. It was then that the coms system started blinking. He wasn't sure he wanted to, but he reached over and flicked the switch to enable the video connection.

"Hello Wyatt." Sonnet smiled at him from the screen. "It's good to see you."

"Wish I could say the same." He replied, as he started reloading of copy of Al from his wrist com into the main computer system. Al had been purged by Curzo to prevent Wyatt from taking control of the ship remotely. "What's on your mind?"

"Well I was thinking about taking my new ship here, spending a little time figuring out how it works, and then blowing you out of space." She replied a fierce look etched on her face.

"Oh I don't think you want to be doing that." He replied, a most calm, almost disinterested look staring back at her.

"Ma'am!" A crewman Wyatt couldn't see started shouting at her. "The computer is fighting back. I can't gain full control."

She shot him a dirty look to indicate the sin he had just committed. He had given information out that could be used against her. Not, that for one moment, she believed that Wyatt wasn't responsible for what was happening.

"I do not think that would be an acceptable course of action." Came the voice of Al through both coms and internal ship's speakers. "It would be a shame if you were to perpetrate a hostile action against my owner. I might just accidently depressurize the ship at an un-opportune moment, or cause one of the alien reactors to overload. Do you know how to shut down an alien reactor, perchance?"

"What the hell are you trying to pull Wyatt?" She yelled at him, her face contorting in rage. "You know it's only a matter of time before we isolate and delete your AI."

"Maybe." Wyatt replied. "But it's also just a matter of time before our distress call gets answered."

"We can still maneuver." She growled at him. "We can still activate the forward cutting lasers." She called up some of the ship's schematics she had found to let him know that she was being truthful. "I can still cut your ship into little pieces and leave you drifting helpless in space or worse."

"We're already drifting helpless in space." He shrugged. "Kenjay did a masterful job of sabotaging the engines. It's going to be sometime before we can get underway."

A calming look and devious smile of admiration then crossed her face.

"Then I propose a truce." Sonnet replied, her composure returning.

"Go ahead. I'm listening."

"You delay your distress call until we are underway. I'll leave you intact. I have no reason to kill you now." Truthfully the only reason to kill him now would be to continue to look for the *Rose*. Something she couldn't afford to try to do in this unfamiliar vessel, nor did she have the crew required to launch any kind of salvage operations. Now her only chance of getting the *Rose* was to return to civilization, attempt to raise a new crew, and return before Wyatt could. And they could and would be years searching the asteroid field for the *Rose*, if it was even here. On the other hand, she now had a new and powerful ship under her command. One that would fetch a high price for its alien technology. If she didn't decide to keep it and use it to plunder other vessels. No, the *Rose* was a gamble, the alien ship, was a sure thing. It wasn't a hard decision to make. "All you have to do is give me the code to delete your AI."

"And what kind of guarantee do I have you won't cut us to ribbons, once you have full control of that ship?" Wyatt gave her a look of distrust, but truthfully, he had few options. He *might* be able to fix the ship before they figured out how to bypass Al. But if he failed, she would destroy his ship and everyone on it.

"I'll tell you what." He began. "I'll put Al on a time delay. He will delete in a standard week. That would give the Space Corps time to respond to our distress call. And it will ensure that you don't stick around and kill us."

A look of concentration crossed her face. She was weighing options, of which she didn't have many either. She could hang around, try to delete his AI and hope she could do it without the AI blowing up the ship, or she could trust him and retreat. She could then return with a crew large enough to continue to search for her quarry.

"Order your AI to obey my commands, and I'll agree to your terms." She finally spat.

"AL!" Wyatt called out and awaited the proper response from Al. "Obey all commands from Sonnet, that will not cause me any harm or interfere with my interest, and acknowledge her as your captain. Standard deletion protocol one standard week from now. In one week, you will delete all personality protocols and become a generic operating system, answerable to Sonnet. Command authorization, Alpha, Lima, Foxtrot, three, seven, niner."

"Command acknowledged." Al replied, with a cyber sigh. "It was a pleasure working with you."

"Al," Sonnet called out to her new AI. "Status report. Readout only, on screen." Sonnet's eyes went wide as she read down the list of items the ship contained and what it could do. She especially was struck when the alien crew roster came up and she realize she was now carrying actual aliens, and she wondered what they could bring on the black market.

"I expect you'll be leaving now." Wyatt called her attention back to him.

"You are most correct." She smiled at him. "We have much to do. It was a pleasure working with you Wyatt. Let's not do it again."

"Likewise." Wyatt then cut the connection and watched his screens to make sure the alien ship left them alone as promised.

"So we have nothing." Kenjay griped, surprising the marshal as he hadn't even been aware that the sword master had been up and about. "It would have been more honorable had I died."

"I wouldn't say we have nothing." Wyatt replied with a grin. "Kirby." Wyatt called out over the coms. "Can you come on over and give us a tow?"

"Sure thing buddy." Came Kirby's familiar voice over the coms. "I'll be there in five."

CHAPTER 36

Kirby's version of 'over in five' actually meant five hours. Wyatt passed the time by getting some food in him, for it had been a week since he had last eaten. He then used a hover lift to move the bodies out of the bay and into a secured storage container. One that would seal properly. All of them except for Green, who he treated with much more care and respect. He did, however, have to put her into storage as well. Except hers was much more pristine and she was by herself.

It turned out, much to everyone except Wyatt's surprise, that Kirby had been piloting Wyatt's ship, the *Stallion,* and had it cloaked and slaved it to the controls of the *Revenge*. That way any maneuver one ship made, the other would mirror and look just like a sensor echo or shadow. Wyatt had also had the *Stallion* dropping buoys or breadcrumbs along the way on a special frequency that only he should be listening to.

The laser that slaved the ships together, also acted like a microphone, so Kirby could keep tabs on everything going on onboard the *Revenge*. When he heard the bridge crew, discussing finding the *Rose*, the phrase 'easy as pie' struck a chord with him. Kirby then used an algorithm, based on PI to analyze the asteroid belt and find the prize. He then used the construction pod that Wyatt had given him to lay a camouflage webbing over the ship to hide it from anyone else. To anyone else's scanners, the *Rose* looked just like any other part of the barren asteroid on which she was parked.

"It is sure good to see you Kirby." Wyatt breathed a sigh of relief as the two met on the bridge of the *Stallion*.

"I sure had my doubts about you when I saw what a mess you made of that fine ship." Kirby laughed as he referred to the damage on the *Revenge*. "It's a pity that lady got away with that other vessel. Not only would I have loved to take a gander at her, I don't like the thought of her running around the galaxy in a ship that powerful."

"Oh she won't be running around for long." Wyatt winked at his friend.

Everyone on the bridge was both dumbstruck and curious about what he meant by that little nugget. They all silently bade him to continue.

"Do you remember what the law says will happen to people that try to hide alien technology?" There were nods from all around him, so he continued. "As soon as Al deletes the personality parts of his program an announcement will be go out from the ship, outlining who and what is onboard, where they are, and the fact that they took the vessel from a law enforcement official who was just trying to bring it to the proper authorities. How do you think the Space Corps are going to respond to that?"

There were hungry smiles from around the room. Attempting to hide alien technology, or dealing with it on the black market, was punishable by death. The governments of both humans and Samurai/Samrazi alike were terrified of running into another alien menace. All alien technology, no matter how small, had to be turned over for study. Having an entire ship, complete with alien bodies on board, was going to earn Sonnet a heap of trouble. She would probably be charged with treason.

"One other little tidbit that might satisfy the more punishment minded among us." He looked over at the slowly healing Kenjay at that. "There is no food aboard the ship that Sonnet took from me. They are going to be at least a week getting anywhere where they can resupply too."

Everyone laughed at that little nugget. It was sure to be an unpleasant trip back to anywhere that they could provision.

"Well I guess it's about that time." Kirby grumped. "If you'll all excuse me I've got to go look at what Master Kenjay did to the engine control computer on the *Revenge.*"

"We should probably go with you." Oso pipped up, indicating himself an Annwyl. "There may still be the body of a crewman down there. We, uh, hit him with a pipe."

Kirby paled a little at that, he wasn't a blood and guts kind of guy. By the time he got through all the destruction in the cargo hold of the *Revenge*, he wasn't going to be a happy camper, and the thoughts of bodies being around would probably make him lose his appetite for a while.

It took almost a week to fully survey the wreck of the *Western Rose*. There was cargo to inventory and manifest. Items of claim to transfer to the *Stallion* so that even if the *Rose* had to stay behind they could present proof of finding her. As it would turn out, that would not be the case. Kirby had launched a hyper buoy announcing the discovery and his and Wyatt's claim on the vessel, the moment he had complete sensor readings on her. By the time Wyatt and his crew had completed the survey of the wreck, representatives from Well Argo had arrived to assist.

With the original transport company on board with the salvage, the amounts the crew would receive were diminished by quite a bit, but it would still be more than even Annwyl could ever spend at only three percent. Wyatt's twenty percent would make him one of the richest men in the quadrant, if not the galaxy proper. Even Kenjay would make out very well, despite being the original owner of the dark matter cargo in the first place. True he lost money on having to pay the enormous finder's fees to Wyatt and the others, but with the banking assets onboard that he would now receive a share of, he more than made up for it.

The reps from Wells Argo also brought a little bit of good news with them. It would appear that an alien ship with three pirates onboard, had been captured, just off of Tortuga. The Navy scooped them up in short order after receiving a computerized message about someone stealing the ship from a lawman attempting to bring it to the proper authorities. That lawman now stood to receive compensation from the government for his find, and the pirates were all being held at an undisclosed location. Needless to say, they would probably never be seen again.

Wyatt sat on the bridge of the *Revenge*, coffee in one hand and the other keeping time to some classical music he had playing.

Kenjay stood in the doorway, watching the complex and honorable man before him. Wyatt was still a puzzle to him, even now. Still he considered the rough and tumble cowboy a true friend. He had saved him. Physically as well as financially. He would owe the man forever. Still there was one thing that puzzled him.

"Wyatt," Kenjay voiced to announce his entry. "Am I disturbing you?"

"Nope." Wyatt drawled. "Just waiting on our permission to leave. Kirby is going to fly back the *Stallion* for me, so you and the rest of the bunch are stuck with me for the return trip."

Kenjay smiled at that. It wasn't like any of them would have it any other way.

"I reviewed the footage of our battle for the ship." Kenjay announced. "It was all captured on the ships scanners and recorded from multiple angles. Your distraction of the fog was ingenious by the way."

Wyatt nodded in thanks, but said nothing.

"I was curious by the fact that you let Fox Pruit go." The Samurai gave the bounty-marshal a quizzical look. "If it is not too personal a question to ask, why did you not take him up on his challenge?"

Wyatt looked absently out the window for a few minutes, just admiring the stars and considering his answer.

"How much do you know about the old west on Earth?" He finally asked his alien friend.

"Just what your people have shown in HD vids and documentaries." Kenjay replied. "It was not exactly a field of great interest to study."

"Did you know that the quick draw showdown, that get shown in the vids, almost never happened?" Wyatt informed him. "Oh there were a couple of incidents here and there, but it was exceedingly rare. That's partly because the fast draws of the west carefully avoided each other."

"Really?" Kenjay was surprised at that. In his culture, the best swordsmen had sought each other out. Looking to claim the title as the best of their clan. It was quite an honor. "I would have thought they would have sought each other out to find out who was the best. To see who was really the fastest gun in the west."

"That's what a lot of people think." He then changed his tact a little. "Kenjay, just how fast do you think I am?"

"I have witnessed you draw and shoot accurately faster than a man can blink." Which was very true. He had personally witnessed that very thing on more than one occasion.

"How fast do you think Fox Pruit is?" Wyatt pressed.

"I would assume that he is of similar ability."

"So if I drew that fast, and he drew that fast, who wins?" Wyatt gave Kenjay a look that told him to stop and consider his answer. Which is just what the samurai did.

"You would both be dead!" He finally realized what Wyatt was talking about. Even a quarter second difference would put their shots in the air at roughly the same time. If they were of equal skill, they would equally kill each other. It was not so, with a sword. At least examples of where two swordsmen had killed each other was exceedingly rare.

"And if we were both dead, who would fly the ship? Who would have finished dealing with Sonnet, and who would have taken care of you?" Wyatt riddled.

"Are you saying you endured the humiliation of walking away from that fight in order to save your crew?" Kenjay was in shock at that revelation, and slightly in awe of it as well.

"Oh there was a tad bit of genuine fear in that decision as well." The marshal assured him. "But mostly I was worried that if I lost to Fox, you would all lose as well. And that would be worse than death."

Kenjay nodded in understanding and appreciation. Still there were many questions running around in his head.

"Are you afraid to die?" The sword master asked quietly.

"I don't know if fear is the right word." He mused in reply. "Let's just say I'm not looking forward to it anytime soon."

"I believe I understand what you mean." Kenjay replied, rubbing his still healing chest.

The two friends then sat there in silence for a long time. Each musing over their own mortality, and each realizing just how much more they now had to live for.

THE END

CHARACTER LIST/INFORMATION

Samriza: Alien species nicknamed the Samurai due to their tendency to wear armor that greatly resembled that of the ancient Samurai. They had faces that resembled clay faces of theater and possessed a strict honor code mush like that of the Bushido.

Wyatt Toranado: Goes by Wyatt. Gunslinger, bounty hunter, professional troubleshooter.

Tishora Zakicowi: Criminal, Pirate, Hijacked Wells Argo Transport and hid the booty.

Oso Zakicowi: Son of Tishora Zakicowi. Approx. 13 years of age.

Master Kenjay: Businessman, borderline mobster.

Sonnet Melville: Father disappeared looking for Wells Argo stage.

Wells Argo stage, actually named WESTERN ROSE.

Alexander Kirby: Locksmith, salvage expert, vessel repair expert, and inventor.

Annwyl/Number 4: Slave of Tishora Zakicowi's

S-year: Standard year, agreed upon year of record by the Samrazi and Human races. 400 Earth days long. Humans recognize the 12 standard months plus and extra month called Luna. February is now 31 days long, as is June. Luna is 31 days long to make 400 days.

Curzo: Pirate, and competitor in chasing down the *Western Rose*.

Fox Pruit: Competitor Bounty hunter. Barred from being employed as a marshal.

Made in the USA
Monee, IL
09 October 2021